THE ANCIENT MEDALLION

THE STORY
OF THE FIRST MISSIONARY
POCKET FORMULA

A SPECIAL REQUEST

The response to this story has already been much more enthusiastic and emotional than I ever expected that it would be. However, as it is a new publication, your opinions are very important to me. If you enjoy the story and would like to comment or ask questions, I would greatly appreciate your thoughts. I will answer all letters as soon as possible.

You can address your correspondence to;
Roy Bates
632 North, 900 East
Mapleton, Utah 84664

ISBN# 1-886472-57-2

To the Reader,

This book has only one main purpose. That purpose is to help the reader learn to control and harness the limitless powers of his own mind and its thoughts. The story is meant to be entertaining and uplifting, but is only a means to an end.

Before you begin, it is suggested if possible, that you have one and a half to two hours available so that you can read the entire book completely through. Only by keeping in the rhythm of the story can you feel the complete impact.

It is also suggested that you refer frequently to the representation of the medallion on the front of the book or to your own 'pocket formula' so that you can identify with the teachings of each symbol.

I sincerely hope you enjoy the story, but most of all, I hope that the principles, ideas and techniques that are shared with you help you as much as they have me.

The Author

This book is dedicated to the most beautiful girl in the world and my best friend for the past twenty three years... My wife Chrys.

A SPECIAL THANK YOU

To my father, Dan Bates, who passed away in 1993, but who needs to know that I finally finished this story.

To my mother, Kate W. Bates for giving me the desire to write and for being my number one promoter.

To my seven children, two of whom are now serving full time missions, one who watches us from the other side, and four who are yet to serve in one way or another.

To Eileen Little and Larry Bates who, after reading a rough version of this story, graciously volunteered to be my editors. Their expertise and suggestions were essential to the finished product.

And to Doyl Peck, the publisher and 'Sounds of Zion' for being willing to look through the mistakes and put their confidence in the story and its message.

Every person that sets out to do anything needs to have a clear vision of the end result. For me, it was the mental picture of my book on the shelves of Palmer's bookstore, in Blanding, Utah. I told the owner, Steve Palmer about my story six or seven years ago. He said it was a great idea and enthusiastically encouraged me to get it published. Whether it was because he really thought the idea was good or just because he was trying to be kind doesn't really matter.

But thanks Steve.

...And let virtue garnish thy thoughts
unceasingly, then shall thy confidence
wax strong in the presence of God,
and the doctrine of the priesthood shall distil
upon thy soul as the dews from heaven...

Doctrine and Covenants
section 121, verse 45

CHAPTER 1

Rick Jamison stood on the veranda of the Stake President's home, looking out over Heber Valley, and for a long moment his thoughts were back in Michigan. "It's beautiful there," he thought to himself, "but it sure is good to be home." He looked southwest at the snow-covered Mt. Timpanogos as it reflected in the glassy waters of Deer Creek Reservoir.

Rick's father put his hand on his shoulder and prodded, "Come on son, enough daydreaming. They're going to wonder if we came to see them or if we just came to stand on their porch."

His mother rang the doorbell, and in a moment an older woman answered.

"Come in, come in," she bubbled. "It's good to see you, Bishop, and how are you Sister Jamison? And Rick! My goodness, you've changed, and look how you've grown."

"Well, you haven't changed," he thought smiling. "You still talk to me like I was twelve years old." He didn't mind though. In fact, he kind of liked it. And he loved Sister Jensen.

"Come sit down," she gestured. "I'll call Albert." She turned to the stairs and called for her husband. Then she motioned to the living room on the right where an older woman was sitting.

"Bishop and Sister Jamison, this is my cousin, Elizabeth, from Star Valley." She winked at the older woman as she introduced her. "She is staying with us for the weekend."

"A pleasure to meet you," Rick's mother offered warmly as she crossed the room to shake her hand. "We're the Jamison's. My name is Katherine, this is my husband, Don, and our son, Rick, who just returned from his mission in Michigan."

"I'm delighted," Elizabeth smiled warmly as she replied: "Albert and Louise were just telling me a little about you."

"I hope it wasn't anything bad," Rick joked. He knew that President Jensen knew him better than anyone, except maybe his parents.

"Of course not," she exclaimed, smiling and getting up as if to leave the room.

"Don't get up," Sister Jamison insisted. "We just came to have Rick released as a missionary and visit for a while. Besides, I have a sister who moved to Afton a year ago and you might know her family. Their name is Palmer; her husband is Tom and he teaches at the high school."

That was Rick's mom. She always seemed to know somebody from just about everywhere. "It's a good way to find common ground when meeting new people," she always said, as if to to defend herself when her husband became embarrassed. Rick's father was just the opposite of his mother. He was quiet and reserved, and chose to stay in the background most of the time. "Don't you mind me," he always said. "If something absolutely needs to be said, I'll say it." Members of his ward had wondered when he became Bishop just how he would handle it, but it was almost magic. For that four and a half years you couldn't shut him up. Then, as soon as he was released, he reverted back to being the same quiet person he had always been.

"Why don't you sit with us for a while," Sister Jensen said smiling, gesturing to Elizabeth.

Just then President Jensen came down the stairs. He was a big man, built like you would think a rancher should be, broad shoulders, a barrel chest, huge muscular arms and hands as big as bear paws. He had red hair that was just beginning to turn gray and a ruddy face that looked like it was born smiling and then froze that way.

"Good to see you Rick, my boy," he boomed. "You look well fed; in fact you look fattened up and ready for market." He poked Rick in the ribs good naturedly as he chuckled.

As a matter of fact, Rick was a good twenty pounds heavier than he had been when he left. That was a very sensitive fact to him, and one that was not lost on his girlfriend, Kristi. She had made a special point to tease him about it as they were walking with his family in the airport earlier that day.

President Jensen had always been one of Rick's favorite people. He remembered how excited he was when he read the letter his dad had written, telling him that Albert Jensen had been called as the new Stake President. He remembered well the time he spent working summers on the Jensen ranch, hauling hay and feeding cattle. More than anything else, he had always admired the way he could put people around him at ease so quickly.

"There were few enough people in the world," he thought, "that were both noble enough to inspire the best in others and humble enough to be approachable."

President Jensen was all of that, and had a wonderful sense of humor as well. He had always been gentle and patient with Rick, even when he had messed up and caused them both extra work. Rick had made up his mind long ago that the perfect man, if there was one, would have a little of his dad, a little of his grandpa and a little of President Jensen in him.

"So you want to get released to go challenge and testify to the young sisters, do you?"

"Well, kind of," Rick replied sheepishly. "I don't have a date till tomorrow night though."

"Bill Richardson's daughter?"

"Yes." He smiled as he thought of Kristi. Everyone in the Stake knew that they had been dating since the beginning of his senior year.

"Kind of thought so," the big rancher muttered approvingly. "She's quite a catch, that one," he thought out loud. "Feisty, just like her mother; You sure you're man enough for her?"

"I think so," Rick said, sounding a little embarrassed.

President Jensen then motioned for each of them to sit down. Bishop and Sister Jamison took a seat on the sofa as Sister Jensen and Elizabeth sat on the love seat. President Jensen waited until Rick had seated himself on one of the two wing-back chairs by the window, and then he sat down in the other one.

The Stake President then took a letter from the top of the piano and opened it.

"With your permission, Elder, and you are still an elder for the time being, I would like to read to you and your parents this letter from your Mission President. Would that be OK?"

"Of course," Rick answered.

Dearborn Michigan Mission
3335 Rotunda
Dearborn, Michigan

Dear President Jensen,

It is with mixed emotions that I return to you and your stake one of the finest Elders that I have had the pleasure of working with. Elder Rick Jamison has been a pure joy for us to have here in the Dearborn, Michigan Mission.

I must tell you, however, that during his first year there were some concerns. He did nothing wrong, I want you to know, but his heart wasn't in his work.

Then a magnificent change came over this young man, just before the end of his first year. Since then he has been the model of consistency and diligence. He has trained four new elders and has done a wonderful job with each of them. One particular elder, an Elder Call, who is now one of our Zone leaders and was one of Elder Jamison's trainees, goes so far as to say that Elder Jamison was the finest missionary in our mission. He has also been working closely with the office during the past two months, helping us implement a systematic program for training new elders.

I asked him a few weeks ago, when we had some time together, to tell me what had sparked the change in his life. The story he told me was nearly unbelievable. You would do well to insist that he tell you the same tale. As far as I am concerned, the results I have seen in him tell me that it must be true. Thanks for the use of this wonderful young man.

Sincerely, yours in the gospel,
President Russell Patterson

Elder Jamison's parents both had tears in their eyes, as did Sister Jensen's cousin Elizabeth. Sister Jensen just looked pleased.

President Jensen looked over at Rick with a smile and said, "I've got a bit of an idea what he's talking about, so Rick, if you and your folks don't have to be anywhere for a little while, why don't you tell us the whole story."

Rick looked first at his parents and then replied, "Well, I figured that I would tell you tonight anyway. I started to write to you about it a dozen times but I never did feel comfortable putting the whole story out there in print the way that it actually happened. I was afraid of how it might sound, and crazy or not, I think it's the most sacred and special thing that has ever happened to me."

"It is important for you to know that President Patterson was right about my first eleven months, even though I would have rather he not be so honest with you."

He smiled as he continued.

"The fact is, I felt like I was walking in knee deep mud from the moment I got there. Right from the start everything seemed to be different from what I had expected. I had thought that people would be lining up at the airport to have me escort them into the waters of baptism.

"Well, truthfully, I wasn't quite that far off, but there was a major difference between my expectations and reality. I quickly learned that finding people to teach took hard work and inspiration.

"I really don't mind hard work. In fact I remember you and dad teaching me, President, that giving a hundred percent is usually much easier than trying to get by with less. I guess I just lost sight of that for a while.

"It's kind of like a football player who trains all summer with no grasp on reality. Without anyone to test his skills against, he convinces himself as he continues to see improvement, that he is all-American material. Then when the Fall practices start and the hitting begins, and his skills are put to the test, he finds that he is not only not an All-American, but that he is assigned to the third string. Sometimes instead of re-committing and trying harder, he chooses to either give up altogether, or sit and pout and feel sorry for himself."

The stake president was grinning and his father looked proud.

"Well, that is exactly where I was. I had let my memorization slip, my scripture reading was erratic at best and my work habits just weren't good at all. I was doing my best to just sort of slide by.

"I felt awful about everything and I knew I had to make a change. I kept thinking that everything would turn around and that something would happen that would provide the spark to get me started. Problem was, the time just kept slipping away. Then something did happen."

CHAPTER 2

It was last year, just before Thanksgiving and I was serving in the Fenton-Holly area.

Elder Mitchell and I had just gotten home that evening from a discussion when the phone rang. When I picked it up, I was surprised to hear President Patterson's voice on the other end.

"Elder Jamison?" he said.

"Yes?"

"Elder, this is President Patterson calling. How are you doing?"

"Fine, President," I stammered. "How are you?"

"I'm doing great, Elder. Are you in the middle of anything? I need to discuss a matter with you if you have a few minutes."

"No, we're not doing anything. We just walked in the door from a discussion." I always wanted him to know, or at least think, that we were busy.

I was very nervous talking to him. He almost never called unless there was something serious to talk about. I was especially on edge, not only because I hadn't been putting out the right effort, but because I knew that he knew it. I was supposed to have passed off my discussions long before that time, but had successfully dodged each opportunity. I guess it was mostly because I knew what my pass-off report would look like.

Funny thing, though, when I didn't have to speak to

the president or one of the assistants, I still had this mental picture of myself as a leader, albeit one with a guilty conscience. Then every time I was forced to speak to any of them, reality hit.

"Elder, are you familiar with how we go about making transfers?"

"Kind of, I suppose."

He went on. "Every week on Thursday, the assistants and I have a business meeting. In that meeting we discuss, among other matters, who the Lord may want with whom, where they should serve, and should they be training a new elder, that kind of thing. We pray about it during the week as well. Then, usually once a month, based on emergency and when the new missionaries arrive, we do our transfers.

"I want you to know, Elder, that the decisions about transfers are among the most sacred and serious of all that a Mission President has to make."

I was getting pretty scared about that time. Thoughts of receiving a problem elder, staying a junior companion and other fears were going through my head. I knew that I had to receive a new companion of some kind the following week, as Elder Mitchell had just one week left and was going home. I had always assumed that by now tenure alone should make me a senior companion. Now I was getting worried.

"Elder Jamison, I am going to be perfectly frank with you. I don't think that you've shown yet that you can handle the responsibility of training a new elder."

I was offended, and wanted to say, "Well just leave me as a junior companion then, I don't care. I'm doing just fine where I am."

But I didn't.

"The point of this call, Elder Jamison, is to give you a little advance notice. After careful thought and much prayer, we have decided that whether you are ready or not, the Lord wants you to train a new elder. The problem is, that he deserves to be trained by someone who knows his stuff and is excited about the work. We all know that you have the capacity; that isn't the issue. So far, however, it hasn't been used."

Two verses from the Doctrine and Covenants hit me then, with terrific force.

'Reproving betimes with sharpness, when moved upon by the Holy Ghost,' from section 121, verse 43, and

'Whom I love, I also chasten,' from section 95, verse 1.

So I listened.

"What we're telling you is that you have one week to turn things around. I know it will not be easy and I know you can't make up all of the lost ground in that amount of time. But we need you to make the effort. You'll be more or less on your own, you know that. Your companion is thinking more of home at this stage than he is the work, I can tell that just by talking to him.

"Can you accept the challenge, Elder?"

It had already occurred to me that this was the turnaround opportunity I needed. I didn't deserve it, and I knew that, but I needed it.

"Yes, President," I almost shouted. "I'm sure I can."

President Patterson talked to me for a few more minutes after that. The new elder's name was Elder Stevenson, or at least that's what I remembered him telling me.

After he was done, as a final note, he said quietly, "Elder?"

"Yes?"

"If there is anything that I or the assistants can do to help you get ready, let us know. I love you, Elder Jamison, and I have complete confidence in you; I want you to know that."

And I knew that he meant it.

Then I thought,

'And then showing forth an increase of love toward him whom thou has reproved. . . .'

I was sure that this opportunity had come from the Lord, and this time I wasn't going to let him down.

I didn't sleep much that night, which was Thursday, nor did I sleep much Friday night. For the first time, maybe in my life, I started to think about the enormous responsibility it was to be someone's 'first exposure.' Remembering my own first companion, I realized that a good share of the attitudes this new elder would take with him during the next two years would be shaped by his experience with me.

It was terrifying to realize that the one thing I did not want him to become was what I had been.

Elder Mitchell wasn't much help either. At least two or three times each day he would say something like, "They sure are hard up for trainers," or "You can teach him everything you know. . . in about ten minutes." He thought he was being funny, and I suppose that under other circumstances, I would have thought so, too.

The sad part, however, was that he was right.

So that Saturday I decided to fast.

I had not had an honest fast since I arrived in the mission field. Oh, I had cut out two meals in a row, dutifully. And I had worn the 'hungry face' to church the next day. But I had not had a real, pleading, praying, pondering, and searching kind of a fast. This time I was determined to do just that.

Right after breakfast, I went into the bedroom and knelt down and asked the Lord to help me. I put the whole problem before him and held nothing back. It felt good.

Then at lunchtime, while Elder Mitchell fixed himself a sandwich, I went again to the bedroom. Once again, I went through the same process. This time the conversation seemed easier and I stayed on my knees afterward for a few minutes, just thinking.

We finished up our proselyting early that evening and I asked my companion if he would excuse me for the rest of the night. I laid down and turned my Book of Mormon to Third Nephi and began to read. I remember reading about the murder of the chief judge. Then thoughts of what my new companion would look like took over.

It must have been only about nine when I fell asleep.

I don't remember ever sleeping that soundly.

CHAPTER 3

The next thing I remember was a rough, but pleasant voice.

"Wake up, you two," the man insisted.

I turned and saw an older man, maybe in his early sixties, dressed in an ancient robe, standing just a couple of feet from me. Then I saw someone stirring on the ground on the other side of him.

"Elders, the sun is already up and we've got a full day ahead of us," he said.

I had to rub my eyes several times to believe what I was seeing. I was lying between two wool blankets, in a clearing just twenty or so feet from a beautiful pond. I looked beneath the top blanket and could see that I was wearing a robe similar to the old man's. The clearing we were in was surrounded on three sides by a grove of junipers, with cattails and mesquite growing in and around the pond.

On the west, the mountainside came all the way down to the edge of the pond. To the east, between the trees, the clearing emptied into a large valley, with the sun just above the far horizon.

The man who had spoken walked to the edge of the pond and began splashing water on his face. I turned to see who the other person was and saw another young man lying on the ground, not more than ten feet from me. By the look on his face, he was just as surprised by his surroundings as I was.

"Where am I?" he exclaimed. That was the first question on my mind as well.

The older man turned with an impish smile.

"I don't know why I take so much pleasure in seeing the first looks on you young men's faces," he chuckled.

"I am Seth and you are in my camp. Together we are in the central part of the land of Nephi. A few of our guests have taken to calling it the Missionary Training Camp or MTC. I kind of like that name; it fits.

"We need to get moving, though, so if you can get your beds rolled up quickly, we can talk more as we walk."

As I rolled up my blankets, I turned to the other young man and said,

"My name is Elder Jamison, Rick Jamison."

"And I'm Elder Chris Stevenson; good to meet you."

"That's it, I'm dreaming," I thought. I remembered that the last thing on my mind before I fell asleep was my new assignment and my new companion.

"Do you suppose we are dreaming?" he asked.

"Yeah, I'm sure of it. There is no other way to explain any of this."

After we had rolled up our blankets, Seth took them and tied them to the back of one of the three donkeys he had tied to a juniper tree. We each put on the sandals he had given us as we watched him gently stroke his animals. He then took two small round loaves of bread from one of the packs and handed them to us. He also handed us each a handful of dried fruit. Then, gesturing to us and turning on his heel, he led the donkeys to the south of the clearing where the trail went into the trees along the base of the mountain.

The other elder looked as hungry as I was and we both ate our food accordingly. The bread tasted alot like the sourdough that the sheepherders used to make and was good.

As soon as he could see that we were finished eating, Seth turned to us.

"The trail is wide enough that we can walk abreast of each other for awhile, so as we walk, I'll explain a few things to you."

As we fell into step with him, he began.

"First of all, I am not from your time. I guess that's quite obvious to you by now. I am Seth, as I said before, and I am a Missionary Trainer. I, along with my two associates, have been called to train a select group of missionaries. Samuel, who is one of the other two, and I began several years ago at Nephi's request. Then, after Nephi's son, Jonas, returned from his last mission, Nephi asked him to join us, which gave us our third trainer.

"We have trained dozens of missionaries from our time who are now serving and some who will soon be called to serve. We have also had in our classes, many from the last days like the two of you. In fact, my classes, which I usually conduct while moving from place to place, have been almost entirely attended by elders from your time. You may be tempted, like the others, to question why you were chosen for this experience, and frankly, the specific reasons have never been given to me. What I do know is that you both have critical missions to perform that will require the ability to teach others what we are going to teach you."

Elder Stevenson and I looked at each other as we listened.

"In the past, I have conducted my classes mostly north of here. Samuel has had his right in his own village, which you will see, and Jonas has kept his students at his father's house in Zarehemla.

"This time, however, because you two are our only students, we will be sharing in your training. You are very fortunate to be able to learn from these other two wonderful men.

"You will probably notice as we travel and meet others that they will appear to be speaking the language you speak. That is not the case. Everyone here is speaking their own tongue, and you Elders will also be speaking our language. It will not sound like that to you, nor will what we say sound different to you, but it is because you have been prepared to communicate freely with us, at least as far as our language is concerned.

"Now elders, I will explain to you what we are going to be doing and the rules that I expect you to follow.

"The first rule is this: You are free to discuss between yourselves any topic that we are discussing together. In fact we would encourage that. You are, however, to eliminate from your conversation, any discussion about the specifics of your own time and place. All you need to know is that you are from the same dispensation and from roughly the same area. The times from which each of you came could vary from five or ten, to over a hundred years apart.

"Elder Jamison, you are from a later time than Elder Stevenson, so for obvious reasons, you are to be especially careful not to mention events that pertain to your generation.

"Secondly, I would encourage you to pay close attention and to remember all that you can, as you will take nothing back from here except your memory. We will try to cover everything at least twice, sometimes from different angles and sometimes not.

"Do you think you can live by those rules, Elder Stevenson?"

The other Elder responded, "Yes, I think I can."

"And you, Elder Jamison?"

"Certainly."

I would have thought that the strangeness of what was going on would have had me shaking my head for quite a while, but everything seemed right. It's hard for me to explain exactly why, but I felt completely comfortable with my surroundings and with our instructor.

Seth then took two coins or medallions out of his sack and handed one to each of us. They were about the size of a silver dollar and looked gold in color. I turned it over in my hand and looked closely at mine. On the front was a hexagon. Between the circle of the medallion and each of the six sides of the hexagon was a word, written in a language I had never seen. Within the hexagon was a triangle with a word written on each of the three sides. In the center was a likeness of the Sun. I turned it over and on the back was more writing, which of course was strange to me as well.

"We will have you for about twelve days," Seth resumed. "In that time we will discuss everything symbolized on that coin. I will train you on these points so that you can train others when you return." He then stopped and turned to face us.

"We will not be teaching new doctrines or history, nor offering prophecies on the future. We are not prophets, just teachers. We will be discussing principles, techniques, ideas and methods of self development. All laws and doctrines are left to the prophets to expound on.

"So, are you ready to begin?"

"Yes," was the reply from both of us.

It was mid-morning and the sun was about half way up in the eastern sky when he began.

"Elders, the human mind is a wonderful thing. It is

the gate by which all thoughts must pass, both good and evil, both noble and base, before they can manifest themselves as habits, character traits or wisdom. The biggest challenge faced by mankind since our first parents partook of the fruit, has been, and always will be, the control of what is fed to and digested by our minds.

"Also, just as our minds are expert at taking images and translating them into physical reality, they are excellent filtering devices as well. This means that a thought that crosses your mind need not stay there. You, at times, have no choice about what thoughts make an appearance, but you have complete control over which ones remain.

"An evil man does not become an evil man because one evil thought crossed his mind by chance one day. Nor does a prophet become a prophet because a single noble or visionary thought made its mark a single time.

"They each become what they become because they consciously choose to dwell on those particular kinds of thoughts. Then, after a period of time to become familiar with them, they invite similar and relating thoughts to join, eventually building an army of either good or evil thoughts."

Seth continued, "Now I must warn you, however, that when this army of thoughts has become large enough, you no longer have any control of it, for it controls you.

"If you have let your army of evil thoughts grow strong enough, you have no choice but to become evil. Your accumulated thoughts have matured into vile habits and unrighteous character traits that virtually destroy any noble thought you might have, before it can gain hold in your heart.

"Likewise it is with noble or righteous thoughts. Constantly adding righteous thought to righteous thought builds an army that manifests itself in virtuous habits, noble deeds and kindly behavior. Just like the army of evil thoughts can destroy a noble aspiration, so the righteous army, now developed into noble character, causes evil thoughts that try to enter to wither and perish immediately.

"Fortunately, though the door to our mind is always open, it is only wide enough for one thought to enter at a time. That is the way we were created. The reason was to protect us and give us control. If that is so, and it definitely is, then the secret to building a noble army of thoughts is to keep the door continually blocked to evil thoughts by maintaining a steady, unbroken string of pure and righteous thoughts passing through. If an evil thought does try to squeeze in, it can be pushed away quickly.

"The understanding of this principle is what inspired the use of the medallion you hold your hand. On it are represented six of the most essential virtues that you should pursue, the three-step process of developing those virtues, your central point of focus, and a verse to inspire and motivate you. You should keep it with you always, as a reminder of where to direct your thoughts."

We both understood and were nodding in agreement.

"If you can learn and perfect all that is represented on that medallion, you will have won life's most important battle."

We spent the remainder of the morning and the early afternoon discussing the power of righteous thinking. Then, after a brief stop to eat, Seth began his training.

CHAPTER 4

"We will begin by first drawing your attention to the center of the medallion. You will notice that it is a likeness of the sun. I ask you both, what is the meaning of that likeness?"

Elder Stevenson replied, "I would think that it is a reminder of the Savior or the Son of God."

"That's right," Seth agreed, "but it's more than that. What would you say, Elder?" he asked, looking at me.

"Well, I've been taught that all life comes from the sun. Would that be appropriate?"

"Yes it would, and let me explain. Just as all things in the physical world are dependent upon the sun to give them life, so all spiritual life is dependent upon light from the Son of God. It is placed in the center of the front of your medallion to remind you that all thoughts and actions should be centered around him.

"Elders, everything you are going to learn while you are with us is dependent upon the degree that you can keep your 'eye single to his glory.' Everything on your medallion is meant to pull your attention to the sun in the center. Likewise, every virtue that you master and every success that you have should glorify him.

"There is one other thing that we should remember every time we take out our medallions and look at them.

At certain special, sacred times in our life the spirit will seem as strong as the sun is in the heavens in mid-summer. During these times, it seems like the veil that separates the two worlds is almost transparent. All doubts vanish, goodwill abounds and knowledge is fed to our souls spontaneously.

"At other times, when the light dims somewhat to allow us to make decisions on our own, and to give the Lord a chance to see if we can exercise our faith, we need to live in remembrance of what it felt like on that sunny day. We also must live in anticipation that continued right decisions will help us return there again.

"Does that make sense to you, elders?"

We both nodded and replied that it did.

"Then the sun in the center is to remind us to 'keep an eye single to the glory of God.'"

I thought about that for the rest of the morning. It was nothing new. I had been taught that phrase many times.

This time, though, I kept looking at the medallion, and each time my eyes rested on the center I said the words, "Keep an eye single to the glory of God."

What a terrific idea. A coin or medallion that was small enough to fit in a person's pocket, but big enough that a person would not be likely to forget that it was there. I looked at it and then put it back in the pocket of my robe. I then put my hand back in and put my fingers around it. Without seeing it, I could feel each image. I felt the small likeness of the sun in the center and immediately thought again, 'keep an eye single to the glory of God.'

For the next half hour or so Seth remained silent. Occasionally he would look over at each of us and nod in approval, as if he knew exactly what was going through our minds.

What was going through mine was guilt. "What a waste," I thought. "All these last eleven months and most of it wasted. If I had only taken it upon myself to work and study and pray like I had the last couple of days, what effect could I have had on some of my investigators or my companions? There were virtually eleven months of uninspired, 'going through the motions,' behind me."

I thought sadly to myself that there probably wasn't a single person who would say, if asked, that I had made a difference in their conversion.

A few moments later, I was forced to put those thoughts aside as Seth asked, "Elders, I would like you each to think for a minute and then tell me what it means to 'have an eye single to his glory.' I'll give you a minute as we walk and then Elder Jamison, you go first.

"As part of your response, I would like you to answer this. If a person has an occupation that requires his focused attention, and that occupation, by necessity is temporal, how then can he keep the 'glory of God' as his focal point?

"You see, for most of us, that is a valid question. You, as missionaries, have the luxury for the time being at least, of having only one thing to focus on each and every day. You have no money worries, no family responsibilities, really nothing to occupy your attention other than the Lord's work. Cherish it while you have it, elders; don't waste a single precious moment of this wonderful gift.

"However, assuming things take their natural course, within a couple of years, you will lose that luxury for the foreseeable future. So, in the world that you will then enter, how would you justify this conflict?"

We walked silently, thinking to ourselves for the next couple of minutes.

The one thing that I became aware of quickly, and was to appreciate as the days went on, was that Seth was patient. He was perfectly content, after throwing out a point of discussion, to let as much time pass as was necessary to let us construct an answer. What he insisted we do, was to look inward and think.

After some time I replied, "I would think that it means that regardless of what we are doing, whether outwardly spiritual or not, we need to be in harmony with his gospel."

"That's true, Elder, but it goes further. Elder Stevenson, could you add anything to what he has just said?"

"I think that to have 'an eye single to his glory' would mean that everything one did or said, or planned to do or say, would be with the thought in mind that, based on the knowledge I have, does this help or hinder his work? One would also have to ask, is this the decision that he would make?"

"That's good, Elder. Would you give me an example?"

Elder Stevenson looked pleased that Seth had accepted his definition and then replied, "I am planning on becoming a teacher when I return home. I had considered two other occupations that I very much enjoy, but have chosen teaching because the others don't seem to provide the kind of environment that would encourage righteousness.

"I also think that every time a person enters into debt, he must ask himself if what he is going into debt for is worth the loss of his spiritual freedom. My father, though not a religous man, has told me many times that a person who owes all of his income to debts, hasn't got the freedom to help the poor and needy when he would like."

Seth looked genuinely impressed by his answer.

"I think you two have a pretty good understanding of that. For the next few days, as we talk of other things, think of how they can help you 'keep an eye single to his glory.'"

I would guess, based on the fact that we walked for the entire day, from just after sun-up to sun-down, we must have covered at least twenty miles. The area was beautiful in a desert kind of way. It looked a lot like it does in the southwest, with the bright red sandstone formations, and clear blue, cloudless skies. And it felt like spring always felt there. The morning was cool and the afternoon was quite warm, and the air was much drier than I was used to.

We camped that evening at the first water we had seen since morning. I had noticed very little vegetation as we walked that day, but Seth took us right to a nice little spot with a cool spring that was shaded from the late evening sun by a large rock formation.

He drove a stake into the ground, tethered the animals, and while unloading the supplies, asked us to look around for anything that would burn for the fire.

We gathered a pile of dried sage wood and then sat heavily as he put a fire together. As we both took off our sandals, I took the medallion out of the pocket of my robe and stroked it.

Seth saw me and offered, "The missionaries call the medallion their 'pocket formula.' As far as anyone knows, Alma and the sons of Mosiah were the first to use it. Legend has it that as they each prepared to depart for their missions they fashioned these medallions to remind them of each other and to help them concentrate on those things that were most important to them. I also understand that Helaman and his young army each carried one with them as well."

After we had finished eating, Seth asked us to kneel with him for evening prayer. This was the third time we had knelt together that day. Each time we stopped, once in the late morning and once in the mid-afternoon, Seth would say a blessing on our refreshment and take a few minutes to bring the Lord up to date and ask for his help. Each time we would kneel facing each other and upon saying amen, he would take our right hand in his and put his left hand on our shoulder and say, "I love you" to each of us.

He had the most beautiful way of praying. He used the proper language of prayer as we know it, but he spoke to the Lord the way a ranch foreman might speak to the boss at the end of the day. We could both tell that he knew the Lord well and that he loved him and loved the work he was doing.

Then he looked at us both.

"Before you retire, Elders, I would like you to begin thinking about the triangle surrounding the sun in the middle of your medallions.

'The three sides of the triangle signify the 'Three Degrees of Devotion,' which are Faith, Hope and Charity. Tomorrow, when we get to our destination, we will discuss these."

With that, he said goodnight, and retired.

What a day that had been.

I was lying on my back, trying to pick out constellations in the stars and going over in my mind all that happened.

"Seth," I muttered to myself.

As I spoke his name, I smiled. I really liked him. And I felt completely comfortable in his presence. Maybe he was a product of my dream and maybe he was like he was because of that, but regardless of the reason, he was the perfect vision of what I thought an ancient sage should look like.

He stood about five and a half feet tall, and slightly stooped. He had piercing green eyes that were set deep within his weathered face, and thick gray eyebrows, perched like awnings, atop a wide, prominent nose. His hair was wavy and gray and he probably weighed about twenty pounds more than he would have liked.

He wasn't handsome in any physical sense of the word, but his confidence and gentle, logical, systematic way of communicating made him instantly attractive when engaged in instruction or dialogue. I would find, over the next few days that he could convey the depth and gravity of any subject, and put it forth with optimism and humor.

My mind wandered as I looked beyond the stars in the night sky. I imagined myself in the gymnasium in Athens, sitting in front of Socrates as he posed question after question to dozens of attentive young disciples. I could picture myself, sitting with Plato and Crito, fielding each question, with responses born out of considerable deliberation.

"This must be what heaven is like," I thought. "It's so stimulating and challenging, yet peaceful and non-threatening."

I still didn't have a clue where I was however, except that I was probably in Central America somewhere. At least I thought that, from what Seth had said.

But as different as my surroundings were, and I couldn't imagine them being any more different, I felt good and at peace. My feet hurt and my legs were sore from walking all day, but I really felt good.

I thought my new companion had been asleep, but after twenty or thirty minutes he spoke.

"Elder Jamison?"

"Yes?"

"I didn't wake you, did I?"

"No, I was just lying here thinking."

"Me, too. Elder, why do you suppose this is happening to us?"

"I don't know exactly, but I know I was supposed to be training a new Elder next week."

I felt no need to be anything but completely honest about my situation.

"My mission president called me ahead of time and asked me to prepare, because I really am not ready to be a trainer yet. I think that's why it may be happening to me."

"Well, I just got to the mission field a month ago," he said, "so I doubt if that would apply to me yet."

"I was going to ask you where you are serving, but I guess that that's off limits, isn't it?"

"Yes, I suppose it is."

"I think I can ask you this, though," I suggested. You said you were thinking of becoming a teacher. What do you want to teach?"

"Probably history," he replied. "It has always fascinated me. I like trying to search out the minds and hearts of the famous people that lived long ago."

"Me, too," I offered enthusiastically. "Do you ever find yourself putting a gospel framework around people from the past?"

"Yes," he said excitedly. "In fact, I was just thinking about Socrates."

That was the first time I noticed that we always seemed to be thinking similar thoughts.

Elder Stevenson was one of those people that as soon as you meet them you are sure you've known them before. You know how just the way a person holds his mouth or how he looks at you, you can instantly decide whether you like him or not? Well, the second I saw

Elder Stevenson waking up there in the clearing, I knew we would be best friends.

He was maybe an inch taller than I am, a little more slender, and had a slightly uneven walk. He didn't limp, he just walked a little uneven. He had straight, sandy blond hair, a prominent chin, a crooked smile that was uniquely his own and dancing blue eyes. When he spoke, everything out of his mouth sounded confident, which could have intimidated me I suppose, but didn't.

Elder Stevenson continued, "As noble and true of an individual as Socrates was, I'm sure that if the Gospel in its entirety was presented to him, he would have accepted it, don't you?"

"Absolutely. And what about Buddha and Confucius and Lao Tzu?"

"Boy, Elder, we sure do think alike."

A few more minutes passed and then he spoke again.

"Elder Jamison?"

"Yes?"

"If I had to have a dream like this, I'm glad yours and mine are together."

"Me too, Elder."

"Goodnight, Elder Jamison."

"Goodnight."

CHAPTER 5

We were awakened shortly before sunrise the next day, just as promised. Together we had our prayer and a bite to eat and then Seth read to us from his copy of the writings of Isaiah. As he read, he would stop frequently and expound on different points.

It was thrilling to hear him interpret and talk about things from our day as if they hadn't happened yet. When he spoke of how certain passages referred to the restoration of the gospel and the different events surrounding it, I felt like saying,

"Yes! And it did happen that way."

I caught Elder Stevenson's eye and knew he was thinking the same thing.

When Seth finished, it was about an hour past sunup. What gear we hadn't readied while he was preparing breakfast, he quickly loaded and we were off again.

Soon after we started, we discovered that we had been traveling along the top of a large mesa and we could see as we neared the edge that it overlooked a vast series of canyons. At the edge of the mesa, the trail we were on fell away to the right and was barely wide enough for one donkey. We were forced to ease down along the smooth red rock wall single file, each of us leading an animal. Scared to death, I kept my eyes directed either straight ahead or toward the cliff.

After about three quarters of a mile and nearly an hour, we rounded a corner and saw the most breathtaking little valley, nearly fifteen hundred feet below us. It took the better part of three more hours to cover the remaining distance, winding back and forth against the side, until the trail brought us out, alongside a small stream at the edge of a beautiful orchard. After an entire day of walking in the desert, this looked like Shangri-La.

There were apricot, peach and cherry trees and a couple of fruits that I couldn't identify. It looked wonderful, especially against the backdrop of the red cliffs.

To the right of us as we continued, we saw what must have been nearly fifty acres of corn about a foot high, and a vegetable garden with young cabbages, carrots, and peas, all looking well tended.

The little valley was protected on three sides by the walls of the mesa, and the stream that flowed alongside the trail emptied into a river in the distance that ran along the south end of the valley.

About a quarter of a mile from where the trail entered, and to the left nestled at the base of a cliff, were about two dozen small houses. They were cozy, tight-looking little adobe structures, about sixteen to twenty feet square, and were all arranged in a semi-circle, not more than five feet apart in the front and ten feet in the rear. The front of each was facing the center, where there was a large, bare-earth common area. At each end of the horseshoe, between the last house and the cliff was a two story building, considerably larger than the others, with a window on the second story, overlooking the rooftops. The outside walls of the smaller buildings had no windows and there was a six foot adobe wall between each home.

What a perfect defense, I thought. From either of the

windows in the larger buildings a person could see anyone entering the valley from the south, and anyone entering from the mesa would be visible for hours before they arrived.

As we approached the gate on the west end, a group of youngsters whose ages were probably from five to fourteen came running to meet us.

Then a voice came from the corner of the larger building.

"How are you doing, you Nephite scoundrel," someone bellowed.

"Well, I'll be," exclaimed Seth. "My old friend Samuel."

We saw a tall, older man, who looked like he was at least Seth's age, make his way through six or seven chattering kids.

"It sure is good to see you," he cried enthusiastically, and threw his arms around Seth, nearly smothering him.

"And you, too," he choked.

Samuel stood a good head taller than Seth. He was round shouldered and his arms, though weakened by age, still looked powerful and sinewy. He had muscles everywhere it seemed, and was tanned two shades darker than we were. Bare legged as he was, he looked like an aging distance runner.

"Nephi and Timothy were through here yesterday," he said quietly to Seth. "There has been some trouble to the south and they were going to meet Jonas at the crossing and try to help. They said they would have taken the main road, but were afraid that they would be overtaken, so they were forced to take the cliff trail as you did."

Elder Stevenson and I were not aware of much of what was said between the two men. We had been coaxed into a game with the kids. I had one young boy about eight riding on my back and Elder Stevenson was throwing something back and forth with another one.

When we could get back a little closer to the two, we overheard Samuel say to Seth, "I don't think it will be much longer now. Nephi and Timothy told me of what has been going on in the cities and I have to tell you, I hope it's soon."

"Do you think that we could give these two young elders a roof over their heads tonight?" Seth asked, as if to change the subject when he saw us near.

"Of course," he replied. "But you, my old friend, must sleep with the donkeys." He laughed as he slapped Seth on the back.

It was mid-day by that time and we hadn't taken time to eat. When Samuel saw that we had not eaten, he brought us to the open area in the middle of the houses and sat us there at a large stone table. He went into one of the larger buildings and a few minutes later, he and an older woman I assumed was his wife, came out loaded with baskets of food. The baskets were filled with corn bread, dried fruit, and thick chunks of dried meat. After blessing it, he motioned for us to help ourselves.

It was fantastic. The meat was more tender and sweet than any I had tasted and the corn bread and dried fruit were wonderful. I was tempted to ask them what the meat was, but thought better of it.

When we were through eating, we were expecting Seth to get us back into our discussions again. We were both surprised when he excused himself and said he was going to lie under an apricot tree and take a nap.

It seemed like the whole little village fell asleep at the same time. Elder Stevenson and I were left there looking at each other, neither of us tired, but not sure what to do.

"Do you want to take a walk?" I asked.

"Sounds good to me."

As we passed by the vegetable garden and we could see that the others were out of earshot, I turned to him.

"What do you suppose Seth and Samuel were talking about?"

"I don't know, Elder. I've been trying to place together in my mind what year this might be and I haven't been able to put my finger on it."

I remembered my Book of Mormon footnotes and the years it listed.

"It must be quite sometime after Helaman, because Seth talked about the warriors as if that was before his time. And the Savior can't have come yet, because Seth is still talking about that as a future event."

"Let's listen closely and see if we can figure it out," he suggested. "Seth said nothing about us talking about this time and place."

I agreed.

Then we returned to the historical discussion we had started the night before. We spoke of great people of the past like Julius Caesar, Muhammad, St. Augustine, St. Thomas Aquinas and Joan of Arc. Some, we agreed, probably would not have accepted the gospel. But it was fun to think that others might have.

That became our favorite pastime when we were alone. I was amazed at not only what he knew but how well thought-out his opinions were.

We also discussed between us, as we had done the night before, the meaning of Faith, Hope and Charity. We, of course, had no scriptures to refer to, but by memory we talked about what we knew had been said in the Book of Mormon, the Bible and the Doctrine and Covenants. Elder Stevenson was especially familiar with the seventh chapter of Moroni, which helped a great deal.

He indicated that if he had a favorite chapter in the Book of Mormon, it would be Moroni, seven. In it, he said, not only did Mormon teach a more individual definition of each of these three virtues than had been written of before, but the promise in the final verse, given to all who possess charity, is one of the most profound in all of scripture.

It was very clear, listening to Elder Stevenson, that he not only had more basic knowledge of the scriptures than I did, but that he had spent a considerable amount of time and effort in pondering their meaning. He sure seemed to be a little older than the average nineteen year old elder.

I don't think that the people in the village slept more than about an hour and a half, and when they had all risen, it was Samuel, not Seth who came and got us.

CHAPTER 6

"Elders," Samuel announced, "this part of your training is mine."

He started by taking a medallion out of his pocket which was like ours, only made of silver. He looked at it thoughtfully and then looked at us.

"Take a look at the triangle in the center surrounding the sun. Did Seth tell you what that stood for?"

Elder Stevenson spoke first, "He said it stands for Faith, Hope and Charity."

"That's correct. Do you know what each one means?"

Elder Stevenson answered, "I know what faith means as defined by Alma."

"And what is that?"

"He said that if you have faith, you hope for things which are not seen, which are true."

"That's right, Elder, but faith is much more."

"All together, they comprise, in terms of your growth and development, what is known as the 'Three Degrees of Devotion.' These three degrees or stages are what every idea, principle, virtue or technique that you seek to possess must pass through on it's way to perfection.

"These three words represent not only the attainment of the levels that you must reach, but the force that drives you to the next level.

"If you want to put an action definition to faith, it is to seek or to desire or to begin the process. You will remember that Alma compared the word, or the entire Gospel of Christ, to a seed. That is precisely what it is. Also, every different aspect or part of that gospel is a seed by itself. Faith is the germinating agent or the energy source that gets the growth process moving.

"Now, Elders, as a matter of discussion, faith is the action agent that helps us move from one level to another, but it also describes the first level of attainment in the Three Degrees of Devotion. So for this purpose, faith can be described as:

A confidence in the Plan of Salvation,

(As it applies generally)

"Elder Jamison, can a man stop at the faith level and remain there?"

"I wouldn't think that is possible," I replied.

"And why is that?" he returned.

"Well, because within faith is the seed of hope, and faith cannot be fully realized without discovering the beginnings of hope."

"Excellent answer, Elder Jamison. Now as we walk along by this field of corn, let me use it to illustrate.

"You see that Faith, as we are speaking of it, is a wonderful beginning. But it is only a beginning.

"The laws of nature dictate that if it is a healthy or active faith, it must grow to survive. In other words, just as a seed of corn must push through the earth and become a growing stalk or die, so faith must mature into hope or perish."

He paused for a moment and watched us nod in agreement, and then continued, "Now we will discuss hope. Relating it to faith, if faith has to be sought, then hope has to be learned. Hope relies upon a certain confidence that can only be obtained by sincere prayer, diligent study, thoughtful contemplation, and strict obedience to the principles and laws that have been learned. For this exercise, hope can be defined as:

A confidence in the Plan of Salvation,

(As it applies to you or me, personally)

"Before we go further, Elders, let me emphasize how important hope is in the Lord's plan. It is critical to the conversion process and it is your primary duty to sell that hope to the world.

"Let me illustrate with this analogy.

"Take the seller of goods. If he is proficient and well trained at what he does, he knows that he has three primary sales to make.

"First, he must convince his customer that the product he is selling is of great value. Secondly, he must convince him that he has the means, or can afford his product. And third, he must convince the customer that he is deserving of and capable of using his product.

"If this merchant is the seller of princely robes and he is selling them among the peasants, it is not enough to convince them that his robes are of the finest fabric. Nor is it enough to make them believe his price is fair. He must also convince the peasant that he can become a prince. If that peasant cannot picture himself wearing such a garment, then he will never, and should never, purchase the robe at any price.

"That's the way it is with the Lord's children. If they cannot picture themselves becoming like Christ, or at least becoming like the members of the Church of Christ, they will certainly never join his church.

"Now if the merchant has convinced the peasant that the robe is of the finest quality, and is priced fairly, and that he has the means to purchase it, and has trained him to be a prince, and given him a taste of what being a prince is like, would that peasant purchase his robe?"

"That's quite a sale," I answered, "but I'm sure the peasant would purchase it instantly."

Samuel continued. "OK, now let's assume, that feeling like a prince, he decides to attend a princely feast. If the other princes who are there, knowing that he was once a peasant, and feeling threatened by him, treated him as if he were not a prince, despite his credentials and the princely robe that he was wearing, and refused to acknowledge him, what do you suppose would become of him?"

Elder Stevenson spoke up. "He may be tempted to give up on being a prince."

"That's right," Samuel agreed. "What happens all too frequently is that the peasant who wanted to be a prince gets discouraged and withdraws, frequently taking other potential princes with him. What's more, he becomes resentful of the one who sold him the robe in the first place.

"So those who would join the Church must have a measure of confidence that they will belong and fit in, not only with Christ's eternal kingdom, but with those who are already members of the church.

"So you see, Elders, how empty the merchant's and peasant's combined faith becomes if it is not accompanied by a perfect brightness of hope?"

Again, we both nodded and responded that we understood.

Samuel then smiled warmly, paused a moment or two and then, with sincere emphasis began again.
"Now we will discuss the greatest of the three which is Charity, or by definition, 'The Pure Love of Christ.'

"As it relates to the other two, if faith has to be sought, and hope has to be learned, then charity can only be obtained by sharing.

"Charity can also be described as:

A devoted confidence in the Plan of Salvation,

(A knowledge of one's place in the plan,

and the willingness to share it)

"Elders, are there those in our world that stop at hope and never possess charity?"

Elder Stevenson spoke this time.

"Yes, according to our scriptures, I am sure of it. But it would seem that after a time it would become 'false hope.'

"Good thought," Samuel complimented. "But there are those who do stop here, and in stopping they miss the very purpose of their existence. They never realize how close to true discipleship they came. By refusing to grow, they stop their progress, they begin to wither and then they fall.

"Here is the truly sad part. In order to reach that point, they have already, like the corn, grown to near maturity, which means that at that stage of development, they are much bigger and stronger than if they had stopped sooner. Therefore, when they do fall, their fall is much greater."

"And they almost never fall without bringing down other, younger stalks, or people, with them.

"Now you see that just as a healthy growing faith, by it's very nature, must grow into hope, so hope, if growing and developing in true understanding, must, by the same laws of nature, blossom into the fruit of charity. And the very nature of charity is to share, spreading the ripened kernels of corn over the newly plowed field, thus completing the cycle and beginning again with faith.

"We might fairly use these definitions:

Faith is ............BELIEVERSHIP

Hope is............MEMBERSHIP
Charity is .........DISCIPLESHIP

"Elders, I would ask you to relate this process of growth to everything you do. When you learn something new or are trying to develop a new talent or possess a new virtue, take each task or quest through the three-step action process known as faith, hope and charity."

That night Elder Stevenson and I discussed with each other all that we had learned that day. He had me commit to him to search and study in depth the entire seventh chapter of Moroni, as he assured me that what was taught there would help me understand more fully, especially about the importance of charity.

I had found that even though we couldn't talk about our lives back home, there was an unlimited amount of gospel philosophy that we could and did discuss.

I had also taken it for granted that though I knew that the time he came from was definitely before, it was not all that far from my own. He seemed to be able to discuss the events surrounding the restoration of the gospel and the early leaders of the twentieth century better than I could. In fact, he made reference, during one of our discussions, to something that President Heber J. Grant had said. The way he made the reference, and I can't recall exactly, I was left with the feeling that he was speaking of a time that for him would have been the recent past.

The next morning, Samuel walked with us again, strolling through the corn fields as he re-taught us what he had covered the day before. He asked many more questions this time, searching for ways to help us understand how to teach, rather than just understand, the principles.

He also introduced us to a concept he called the

'transfer of faith,' or the 'transfer of enthusiasm.' He described it as the act of shifting the energy that drives the learning process from teacher to student.

"This is every teacher's goal," he said.

"There is a definite, though not always apparent moment in each successful teaching experience where the bulk of enthusiasm and energy being devoted to the subject matter shifts from teacher to student, or in your case, from elder to investigator.

"You will be trying with all of your might to help a person understand a particular concept and how it fits into the overall message. Then suddenly, the student is absorbing everything faster than you can present it, and they end up still not being satisfied when the day's lesson has come to an end.

"That's when you know you've reached them. And that is what we always pray for because that's when you know that the Holy Ghost has taken over. Elders, teaching begins when you begin, but learning never truly begins until that happens." Elder Stevenson questioned him then; "Do you think that you've been able to accomplish that with us?"

"Oh yes," he smiled. "But in your cases, it was not so much a matter of me transferring it to you as it was in you both just taking it."

He seemed genuinely pleased and satisfied that we understood.

Just as Samuel was finishing his line of discussion, a young man came running up and pulled him aside. They talked for nearly a minute and then Samuel turned to us.

"Elders, we are finished for the time being. Something has come up and I would ask you to excuse me with my apologies."

He turned from us quickly and hurried back to

the houses.

We stayed in the little valley that evening and found through conversation, that about a fourth of the people were either Samuel's children or grandchildren and that there were just six major families altogether. There seemed to be a growing sense of urgency about them as each was busy with a particular task and they talked excitedly among themselves as they worked.

We didn't have a chance to see Samuel again that day, but we did have a chance to talk to one of his grandsons. He went on and on about how great a missionary his grandfather had been and how he had even been chased out of one town in fear of his life. He talked to us freely and didn't seem to know that we were not from that time.

We wondered between us, as we sat and talked a while later, if it might be possible that this Samuel was the one known as Samuel the Lamanite.

"He is about the right age, I would guess," Elder Stevenson observed. "And the Book of Mormon did say that he departed out of the land and was never heard from again."

He continued to think out loud. "Well, let's see, if it is the time I think it is and he was not much older than us when it happened, then he wouldn't be more than sixty five or so now. Yes, it's possible."

When we had a chance to talk to Seth later that evening, I asked him, "Would your friend Samuel be Samuel the Lamanite?"

"Do you mean the one who stood on the wall and prophesied of the birth of Christ?"

"Yes, is he the same Samuel?"

Seth rubbed his chin. "I can't say for sure, you understand. I've wondered the same thing many times. We've been friends for quite a while, but I didn't meet him until about thirty years ago, and I was not there when the prophecy was made. I was on my first mission to the land northward at the time and didn't return until just before the signs were given of Christ's birth."

He continued. "I asked him directly once about that very thing, but he laughed it off and indicated that he wouldn't discuss it further.

"I do know that shortly after that incident is when he brought his family to this place. He has told me that much. We are quite a few days' journey from Zarahemla and with the calling he has had, no one in our cities would have had reason to hear of him. I also know that his life was in danger, as he had offended quite a few important people.

"It is my opinion, and I stress that it's only an opinion, that he probably is the same Samuel the Lamanite you speak of."

That gave Elder Stevenson and I much to talk about that night as we pondered Samuel's teaching of the day.

CHAPTER 7

The next morning, Seth came to our room before daylight.

"Elders," he announced, "we must be on our way. I have the donkeys ready and there is some food for each of you in a sack by the gate."

He explained to us that Samuel had left the afternoon before when a message came telling him of some trouble that Nephi and Timothy were having near the crossing.

"That must have been what took him away so quickly yesterday afternoon," I thought.

"We are heading that way ourselves," Seth informed us, "and we may pass him on his way back. He said if we don't, to wish you both the best and tell you that he is remembering you in his prayers."

Seth seemed to be in much more of a hurry as we began that morning. We made good time to the river and then turned with it and traveled west along the road on it's northern bank. I think he was genuinely concerned and wanted to get to Nephi and Timothy as soon as he could.

We stopped only briefly mid-morning and took just enough time to eat some of the fruit and dried meat that

Seth had brought from the village. As soon as we were back on our way, Elder Stevenson turned and asked a question we had both wondered about.

"Seth, how long has it been since you were shown the signs of Christ's birth?"

He didn't answer immediately. He seemed to be weighing in his mind whether or not to tell us more than we had already gathered. After a short pause, he seemed to come to a conclusion.

"This coming Monday will complete the thirty third year, the way I have it figured."

I thought out loud, "Then that would mean. . . "

"Yes, I believe the time is near. I'm sure you sensed the urgency at the village. Most people who believe in the prophecies feel like it should have happened already. Nephi and Timothy have been warning people to be ready for some time now. That is what they were doing when they came through Samuel's village a couple of days ago.

"That is also why Samuel left so suddenly yesterday. It seems that something has happened to Timothy."

Elder Stevenson looked my way and our eyes met as if we were thinking the same thing. This was enormous, and scary. I tried to remember all of what it said in Third Nephi about the destruction that accompanied his crucifixion. I remembered reading in seminary about the storms, tempests and earthquakes.

Seth could sense our nervousness and he turned to speak.

"Young men, I want you to know that I have been promised that no harm will come to either of you. If you know of what is to happen, and I know that you do because our leaders are keeping excellent records, then you must know better than I do about the coming events. It is important that you keep that knowledge to yourself, as we may be meeting with others during the next few days."

We stopped for about thirty minutes at lunch time. Seth had us tie the donkeys near the river and we rested beneath a large pecan tree. I found myself wishing that I had taken the time to study the Book of Mormon like I should have. I knew that I had read the date that the destruction was to start, but I couldn't remember then exactly when it was.

Elder Stevenson was sitting just behind my left shoulder and, whispering loud enough so that I could hear, but not loud enough to reach Seth, he said, "Four days past Monday, Elder, if the dates are correct. It is supposed to start in the first month of the thirty-fourth year, on the fourth day of the month."

I didn't know whether I was glad that he knew his scriptures that well or not. I then knew when it would start, and I was worried.

I guess he could sense my fear, because Elder Stevenson took me aside as Seth cared for the animals and taught me a very unique game. He called it Facing off. He said he and his buddies used to play it to relieve tension. He had us stand facing each other, with our feet two inches apart, interlocking so that it was his right, my left, then his left and my right, and had each of us lean slightly to the left, leaving us up against each other and leaning slightly backward. Then we rested our fists, turned up and back, on each other's chest with only the top of the hand and the wrist making contact. Then, when he said 'face off,' we were supposed to punch each other in the chest in this manner until one of us either laughed or stepped out of the way. The one that held his ground and his laugh was the winner.

I thought at the time, "What a strange game," but despite the bruises on my chest, it worked, and my anxiety was gone.

As soon as we were on the trail again, Seth resumed our training on the medallion. "Now Elders, I will explain what the six sides of the hexagon stand for. Each one represents a particular virtue that is essential to your growth. These six virtues are Knowledge, Patience, Diligence, Humility, Brotherhood, and Godliness.

"Each day of the week, Monday through Saturday is assigned a specific virtue. On that day, you should focus on improving your measure of that particular virtue, while maintaining the growth you have achieved in the others.

"We will discuss each of these and, where appropriate, list other virtues that support them and add to your growth.

"Let's start with Knowledge, as that is the virtue for the first day of the week.

"Elder Stevenson, explain briefly, if you will, the importance of obtaining knowledge."

He thought for a few minutes and began. "I have read that to truly follow a law, a person needs to understand and have a complete knowledge of that law. I'm sure that the same applies to all things. I would find it hard to expect myself or anyone else to really become a disciple of Christ if we did not have knowledge of him."

Seth added, "So do you think that one's ability to be obedient is limited by how much he knows?"

"Yes," Elder Stevenson replied, "and I believe it is proportional as he continues to grow."

"Then what about the statement that 'a man will only be judged by what he knows;' Doesn't that indicate that what a man doesn't know can't hurt him? Elder Jamison, you answer that one."

"Maybe as far as judgment is concerned," I replied. "But it would only seem fair that if he cannot be damned by something he doesn't know, he cannot be blessed or exalted by it either."

"Good answer, Elder. Those that choose to cease learning are doomed to enjoy only the promises that the knowledge they have acquired entitles them to. Too many times they end up living in fear of what not to do. They become zealots, ending up being spiritually blind and completely out of balance.

"In the pursuit of a greater knowledge and understanding, a person quickly rises above his fears and lives his life with hope and anticipation. So, to become like Christ, as we are all commanded to do, requires that we first seek to learn all that we can about him and the laws and promises that govern his kingdom. Then we must learn all that he has taught through his servants, about how to become worthy to join him there.

As we acquire knowledge, we must also cultivate the virtues of wisdom, which is the ability to know how to use our knowledge, and discernment, which is the ability to know what knowledge is important and should be pursued and what is not."

MONDAY

(Action Statement)

KNOWLEDGE

Today, I will let the quest for knowledge be my focus. I will seek specialized knowledge, for that is how I gain strength. I will seek general knowledge, for that is how I gain perspective. I will follow the learning path that leads to understanding and wisdom. I will keep my eye single to his glory by not wasting precious time studying theories and ideas that have been proven false. I will seek the inspiration of the Holy Spirit as I learn, that the logic that guides me will be his logic, and that what I learn will increase my ability to become like him. I will share what I learn freely, as directed by the Spirit.

"The second virtue, and the one for Tuesday, is Patience. Elder Jamison, how would you define this?"

"Keeping a level head and allowing people to grow and learn naturally," I replied.

"That's good. And you would probably expect that to apply to yourself as well as to others, wouldn't you?"

Elder Stevenson turned to Seth and interjected, "Yes, I would, but that being the case, how then do we reconcile the need to keep pushing ourselves and challenging others, without crossing that line?"

"Excellent question, Elder. First of all, you are right. We all have to push ourselves from time to time to levels past where we are comfortable. This does cause some stress, and truthfully, it is supposed to. Also, if we are to be an effective teacher, we need to find ways to help others push themselves. That is where inspired patience comes in.

"Let me give you another analogy. I don't know if either of you has ever been on a sailing ship and seen the forces at work there, but every ship that leaves any harbor has really only one objective. That objective is to reach it's destination safely and in the shortest amount of time possible. Would you agree with that?"

"Of course," we said together.

"Now here is the challenge. The least stressful state that any ship could be in is sitting still, with sails lowered, in a protected harbor."

He paused for a moment to let us absorb that statement.

"However, in that state it goes exactly nowhere. Does that make sense to you?"

We both nodded.

"To get the ship moving and keep it moving requires someone, usually the captain, making the decision to cause some stress. As the sails are raised and begin to fill with wind, pressure is put on the mast, all lines begin to tighten and water begins to push heavily in opposing directions on the rudder and keel. Then, if the captain is patient, he trims the sails to just the right point and adjusts the rudder precisely, safely squeezing the maximum amount of performance out of his ship. If he becomes impatient and tries to lean too hard into the wind or to carry more sail that the ship can safely handle, he finds himself shipwrecked.

"I'm sure you can both see the correlation, can't you?"

We both nodded.

"It is important to remember that the captain of the ship has spent many years learning how to read the wind and how far he can safely push the ship's hull. For one of the passengers to assume that responsibility would be disaster. It's the same with each individual. Only the Lord knows how to read the winds that are on the horizon and how much each person can take and still move forward. That is why patience is a virtue that is so dependent upon inspiration from him.

"One more thing you need to remember. People are like ships in another way. Some are built to cross the seas with amazing speed and can be piloted to take advantage of that design. Others are solid, strong, beamy vessels, built to carry many passengers and much cargo and withstand heavy weather. They are not capable of traveling at the same speed, but if kept at a safe pace, are capable of withstanding much more severe conditions, and should be captained accordingly.

"Two virtues that you should develop along with patience are persistence, which is the commitment to stay on course regardless of the obstacles, and temperance, which is the ability to keep all things in their proper balance."

TUESDAY

(Action Statement)

PATIENCE

I will persist until I succeed in my calling. I will build upon my successes and not dwell upon my failures. I will try to adopt the Lord's timetable in all things. I will always strive to understand that though never satisfied, I can always be at peace with honest effort and measurable improvement. I will trust in the Lord in all things. I will be tolerant of others. I will learn and practice that though I should never give up, sometimes I must back off. I will seek to inspire rather than control. I will be a good finder. I will show my love for Christ by being patient with all of his children, even myself.

"Now we will discuss Wednesday's virtue which is diligence. This is the habit of doing what needs to be done, when it needs to be done, and how it needs to be done.

"Now let's return to the analogy of the ship. Elder Stevenson, what are some of the duties that a crew member might be asked to perform?"

"Well, there would need to be someone to tend the helm, another to stand watch, one to take readings at proper times, and someone to make sure the sails, hardware and lines remained in good repair."

"That's correct, and Elder Jamison, what would happen if any of these crew members neglected their specific duties?"

"It could put the entire ship at risk during foul weather," I replied.

"That's exactly what the Lord is talking about when he insists on diligence from us. Just like the crew of a ship, if any of those in his church neglect their duty, it puts undue burdens on the entire organization. A diligent crew member pays close attention to all details, even the seemingly small ones. He avoids the temptation to cut corners and realizes that the proven method of doing things is the only wise route to take.

"The virtues that we should seek to support diligence are enthusiasm, obedience, courage and especially the cultivation of righteous habits."

WEDNESDAY

(Action Statement)

DILIGENCE

Today I will be diligent in all that I do. I will serve with passion, courage and enthusiasm. I will go where I am asked to, but am afraid to go. I will do what I should, but am reluctant to do. And I will say what I am inspired to, but am afraid to say. I will pay attention to the little things that I have been counseled to do. I will adhere to all the laws and rules of my calling and fortify myself against temptation by forming good habits. All of this I will do to show my devotion to Christ.

Seth paused for a few moments and then resumed. "Thursday's virtue, Elders, is humility. This is the most commonly misunderstood of all the virtues. To put it simply, it is the willingness to become what God would have you become and to defer to him in all things.

"Before we came to this world, each of us sought and was prepared for a certain task, just like the soldiers in an army are each trained to do specific things and do them with skill and timing. We made a covenant with the Lord, knowing that his vision was greater than our own, that we would accept his counsel and serve him as he saw fit. We can move forward with great confidence and peace of mind if we truly find what it is we have been prepared for and do it, but we will forever be swimming upstream if we continue to insist on counseling him.

"We cannot see the entire battlefield, but he can, and humility is the virtue that allows us to submit to his wisdom in all things. It is also the ability for us to allow his servants who are charged with stewardship over us, to lead us without our murmuring.

"To support the pursuit of humility, we need to possess both the virtue of prayerfulness, which is the willingness and habit of calling upon him regularly, and that of gratitude, which is the magical virtue that, when expressed and shown properly, bonds the giver and receiver forever."

THURSDAY

(Action Statement)

HUMILITY

Today I will become more humble. I will eliminate pride from all that I do. I will serve and, when asked, I will lead, but with the intent to be of service and not to be seen of men. I will pray often and make the Lord part of everything I do. I will express and show gratitude more fully. I will be grateful to the Lord for my struggles, for they make me strong. I will be grateful for my good times, for they renew my soul. And I will be grateful for the times when he delays his answers, for they teach me to think. I will ask the Lord what he would have me be, and then become it.

"Friday's virtue is brotherhood," Seth announced. "As we ponder it's meaning, I would ask you both, would you agree that the power of good is greater than the power of evil?"

"Of course" and "definitely" were our replies.

"Just what is it that makes it so?" he asked.

Neither of us had ever thought that one through. We looked at each other and Elder Stevenson answered, "I've just always accepted that it is, that's all."

Seth then began. "One of the reasons is that there is an eternal law that says that when two evil men band together, there is only the evil power of two men. When ten of them are together, there is the power of only ten men. However when ten righteous men come together in a righteous cause, the Spirit of the Lord becomes the multiplier, thus creating the power of ten times ten, or one hundred. This 'law of righteous brotherhood' is precisely the law that allowed Helaman's young army to prevail against such insurmountable odds.

"The reason is that the very nature of evil is selfishness, which causes all things to ultimately diminish, while the nature of righteousness is to share, thus multiplying and allowing all members to draw individual strength from each other. Hand in hand with brotherhood are the virtues of charity, empathy, kindness, compassion and optimism. All must be obtained to posses brotherhood."

FRIDAY

(Action Statement)

BROTHERHOOD

I am indeed my brother's keeper. As a son of the same Father in Heaven, I owe my brother everything that is within my power to give. I will look at each of my brothers as Christ looks at me. I will seek to always uplift with sincere praise and to diffuse tension with kindness and humor. I will never knowingly allow one of my brothers to be hurt, either by me or by anyone else. I will build him up by focusing on his virtues and assist him with his challenges when asked. Above all, I must remember that service to one of God's own is the only thing that I can ever give back to him that has any value.

Seth turned and faced us and asked, "Can you both see how critical it is to possess these virtues?"

"Yes, we can," we replied simply.

"Then let's discuss Saturday's virtue, which is Godliness. This is the virtue that must possess all others. Each of the other five virtues must be present and must have been obtained by the process of faith, hope and charity, or by seeking, learning and then sharing.

"To develop Godliness you must seek to think as God thinks, observe as he observes, love as he loves and see things as he sees them. All of this must be done with the thought of glorifying him.

"Before any man can lay claim to pure Godliness, he must be willing to achieve that level in the same way Christ did and will. And because he is without sin and is able to give his life freely, and we all have sinned and have no choice but to die, it would seem impossible to achieve that in this lifetime.

"But it is possible, through repentance, to taste of its essence and to possess a sufficient amount of Godliness to assist him as a disciple. Many have achieved a degree of this virtue, men such as Adam, Abraham, Moses, Enoch, Alma, Nephi and others. While keeping our focus on Christ, it is always helpful to learn about these other righteous men and follow their counsel."

SATURDAY

(Action Statement)

GODLINESS

Today I will seek a greater degree of Godliness. I will do this by being of service to all, while observing the possible eternal cause-effect relationship of all things. I will try with all of my heart to think the way he thinks, to do the things he would do, to say the things he would say and above all, to love as he would love. I will commit myself to learn more about him and I will talk to him often. I will enlist the Holy Ghost, who is the tutor he has given me, to help me in my effort.

"You will notice, Elders," Seth said when he had finished, "that there is not a specific virtue for the Lord's day. This day is specifically set aside for thoughtful contemplation, for worship, and for taking inventory of all efforts of the past week."

It was nearly dark when we made camp, and it had been the longest day we had spent yet. I knew I wouldn't remember everything of that day but Elder Stevenson reminded me, "They're all there in the fourth section of the Doctrine and Covenants, Elder."

After we had said our prayers, as we lay there, Elder Stevenson asked me a question.

"Elder Jamison, what do you know of Ben Franklin?"

"Well, I know he was one of the founding fathers, had signed the Declaration of Independence and therefore was one of those whose work was done in the St George Temple. Is there more?"

"The reason I asked was that he used to do the same thing that Seth taught us today. He would concentrate on a particular virtue each day, trying to better himself."

"Well, I guess a good idea is a good idea, wherever or whenever it comes from," I replied.

We continued to talk about Ben Franklin, or rather Elder Stevenson continued to tell me about him until neither of us could keep our eyes open any longer.

CHAPTER 8

We started again at daylight the next morning. As we began I noticed that my legs were getting used to the workout and I actually felt loose and comfortable after only a few minutes. Then, as if we were on a pre-determined schedule, Seth got right into his topic for the day.

"Your final lesson, Elders, is the practice of a particular technique. This should become the vehicle by which all growth in the areas represented on your medallion is sought, learned, evaluated and renewed.

"Through the practice of goal setting, follow through and reassessment, I would like to teach you the secret of 'Growing by the Season' or the magic of compound rebirth. This practice alone will effect the rest of your life as much as any other technique I could teach you."

Seth continued, "The secret to continual growth and development is to keep moving forward and to improve each aspect of your character on a regular basis. Most do this with yearly goals, and it is reasonable to assume that if a person was making regular improvement of any kind on a yearly basis, he would end up far ahead of most.

"The secret to Godlike growth and improvement, however, is to develop the ability to shorten the compounding periods.

"Let me illustrate. We'll assume that you had in your possession one hundred gold coins. If you increased your lot by ten percent per year, at the end of the first year you would have one hundred and ten coins, correct?"

"Yes," we both responded, not knowing where he was going with this.

"Continuing to do that for five years would mean that you would have one hundred and sixty coins. And if you did the same thing for ten years, you would have two hundred and fifty nine coins."

His eyes began to twinkle as he went on.

"Now, if you were to shorten your compounding period to one season, or a quarter of a year, how much do you suppose you would have?"

"At least four times as much," Elder Stevenson returned.

"No, Elder, here's the magic of this process.

"At the end of five years, you would have six hundred and seventy two coins, and at the end of ten years, you would have four thousand five hundred and twenty-six gold coins! In other words, seventeen times more than you would have had under the yearly method."

We both looked doubtful.

"Figure it out Elders, it's all mathematics.

"So you see, if a man could maintain that kind of growth within himself, how rapidly he would ascend through the developmental process."

I was beginning to understand.

"Now, Elders, let's discuss the practicality of this for a minute. Do you suppose that all of your goals, whether set yearly or seasonally, are going to be achieved in the time you planned, or do you suppose that in the course of a lifetime you may have, on occasion, lapses in your progress?"

"Of course, everyone does," I replied.

"That's true," Seth agreed; "and sometimes for very good reason. There are times in our lives when things and events beyond our control take us off course on a particular goal for a time.

"What would happen to you if you set out to accomplish a goal and halfway through the time period it became obvious that it was completely out of reach?"

Elder Stevenson spoke then, "I would probably give up and wait until the next period started."

"Most of us would," Seth acknowledged. "We could re-set a goal for the remainder of the period, but most of us wouldn't. That's one of the main reasons why we should shorten our time frame of accountability. Every time the average man starts a new year, in his mind he begins a new life. So we need to start a new life every season.

"The other side of that coin is that most of us, if we do accomplish our objective early, tend to waste the remainder of the period coasting, and in the process we lose all of our momentum. Remember that any goal, once achieved, no longer motivates.

"Now I will teach you how to apply this technique. I am an older man than you in years and can look back upon my life now with some perspective. What I want to teach you each to do is to work like a young man, but think like an older man." I don't want to discourage you from setting yearly goals, they are still important. All I want to impress upon you is that the time frame you have the most leverage over, while still being long enough to observe true improvement, is the season.

"When you get to my age you should be able to look back and categorize your life by epochs, by periods, by years, and by chapters or seasons. Obviously, that's easiest to do if you planned it and lived it that way.

"So to start with, during the week prior to any season beginning, through study, contemplation, fasting and prayer, you should decide first upon a theme, then upon your text for the season and lastly upon four critical goals.

"The theme is the title or emphasis, that looking back years from now, you would like to characterize this particular season. The text is the particular work that you commit to read during that ninety-day period. Each of the four goals can be anything that has meaning to you and that moves you toward your long-range objective.

"Then, after setting your goals, to be able to hold yourselves accountable on a weekly and daily basis, calculate as if there are only twelve weeks in a given season, rather than thirteen. The reason you should do this is that if you are diligent and accomplish your objective, you will have the thirteenth week for planning, review, taking inventory and re-generation.

"You both understand that all things done in this way should be done in harmony with the constant practice of focusing on your 'daily virtues' each day. You should also keep in mind the action formula behind the 'Three Degrees of Devotion', which is first to desire or to seek, then to learn, and finally to share your expertise and understanding with others.

"Finally, you should always share what you intend to do with someone else. It is important to always have another set of eyes on your progress. Find someone you trust and admire, who knows you and expects the best from you. Keep them informed as to your progress, and give them full freedom to hold you accountable.

"The expectations of those you love and respect can be a powerful tool in your progress. Remember that how we begin any quest is usually based on emotions, but how we finish is based solely on expectations, both our own and those of others."

Seth then changed the topic and instructed, "Now, my young friends, I would like you to turn your medallions over and look on the back. There you will see writing, which you cannot understand and which cannot be literally translated. I will explain it to you as plainly as I can."

"This represents the promise that has been given to all missionaries by the Lord, and it says, as close as I can have you understand";

"If you will let all of your thoughts be ones of virtue, you will have no reason to fear, for the Lord will give you knowledge and understanding, sufficient for your needs."

"What a wonderful promise," I thought. I continued to ponder its implications in my mind as we took a few minutes to stop for lunch and to water the animals.

We had just started again when Seth spotted a small band of five or six Lamanites moving along a trail on the top of a ridge on the other side of the river. He quickly turned us off the road and we caught another path, on top of the mesa about a mile west, that he said ran parallel to the one we had been on. We kept on in that direction for the rest of the day.

Just about dusk, he turned us back toward the river and we made camp just a few hundred feet through the trees from the mesa's edge. While it was still light enough, the three of us left our camp and walked to the edge overlooking the river. Looking out, we could see for miles both to the right and to the left as well as a good five miles beyond the river.

He explained to us about the battles that were going on at that time between the believers and the non-believers. Most of them really weren't battles at all. It was more like the non-believers persecuting and sometimes killing the believers and the believers trying to stay out of their way.

Occasionally some of the righteous did fight back, however, when it became clear that their families were in danger. Apparently that's what had happened to Nephi and Timothy. A band of robbers had surprised them and, knowing that Nephi was the Prophet, and seeing they had an advantage, they fell upon them to slay them.

They took up what they could to defend themselves, and Jonas, who was on his way to meet them, came upon them just as the fighting began. He was carrying a sword and rushed to help. Together, after a short skirmish, the three of them drove off their attackers. In the process, however, Timothy was gravely injured. He had been struck by a club just as the band was retreating. The blow had knocked him from the ledge he was standing on and he fell several feet.

Seth looked at us and confessed, "The messenger that came for Samuel the other night said the injuries inside of him were so severe that they didn't think he would live."

Seth said he feared that the band we had seen earlier may have been the same one that attacked Nephi and Timothy. For that reason, he said, he had taken us on the mesa trail.

He scanned the area for a few minutes until he spotted what he was looking for. He pointed below us, to a trail that left the river just a few hundred feet downstream. It turned nearly ninety degrees and headed southeast as far as we could see.

"That trail leads to a Lamanite city, about a half a day's journey away," he mentioned.

Seth then pointed to a spot on the trail, on the far side of a grove of pinions, and we saw the six of them as they reached the open area. They were heading southeast.

"That's good," he muttered relieved. "It wouldn't do to have me getting you two into a fight you have no part of. And we need to get back to the river road. I think by tomorrow we should meet up with Nephi."

We dusted ourselves off and turned and headed back to our camp.

As we entered the clearing, we could see that there was already a fire going. Cautiously then, Seth looked around the edge of the clearing to see who might have been there. Nothing was missing or disturbed. Our supplies and our animals were all where we had left them.

Then we saw a familiar figure come through the trees with a load of wood under his arm.

"It's good to see you alive and well, Brother Seth," Samuel exclaimed.

"It's good to see you, too," Seth replied, relieved to see that it was Samuel. "But I thought you were with Nephi and Timothy."

"I was," he said excitedly, "and that's quite a story. I'll tell you all about it as soon as we eat. But first, did you see those men up-river? I saw them heading back this way and that's why I hid up here on the bluff."

Seth replied, "Yes, we spotted them earlier in the day and moved up to the mesa trail for the rest of the afternoon."

A few minutes later, as we sat together eating, Samuel began.

"It was the most wonderful thing I have ever seen," he exclaimed. "When I left the village I made very good time. I passed those six thieves the first time just below here, and managed to stay among the rocks and trees until they passed. Still, it took me only about a day and a half to reach Nephi's camp.

"When I arrived, it looked like I had come too late.

Jonas was there, sitting with his head in his hands. When he looked up and saw me, his face was a blank stare."

"'He's dead,' he told me. 'Uncle Timothy is dead.'

"His body was lying in the shade, just behind Jonas.

"'Father has been back in the trees praying since last night,' he moaned.

"Just then I saw Nephi come through the trees and walk toward me.

"Thank the Lord you are here, Brother Samuel," he whispered as he embraced me. He looked long and deep into my eyes, then he looked over at Jonas. After a long moment he motioned for Jonas and I to follow him to where Timothy's body was lying.

"He then tenderly put his hands on Timothy's head and began to speak.

"I can't remember exactly what he said, but I do remember that he talked for a few minutes about the things that his brother was still supposed to do. When he was nearly finished, he said confidently, 'And in the name of Christ, I command you to arise and live.'

"Immediately, Timothy opened his eyes. He sat there for another couple of minutes and then he got to his feet and embraced all three of us."

I looked over at Elder Stevenson and he was wide eyed.

Samuel continued.

"They are only a few hours' journey from here. I'll take you there in the morning. We can be there well before noon."

When I could get Elder Stevenson alone for a minute, I asked him excitedly, "Do you know who Timothy is?"

"No, Elder, who?"

"He's the brother of Nephi, who he raised from the

dead, who also was one of the twelve disciples in Third Nephi. He and Nephi are the only two whose names I remember."

Elder Stevenson was excited.

And I was thrilled to finally remember something he didn't!

That night we knelt together, the four of us, in a strange land, nineteen hundred and sixty-five years ago, and I heard Samuel talk with God. I know we were on our knees for over an hour and the language Samuel used we only partially understood. But both of us felt positive that if we had opened our eyes we would have seen angels kneeling there with us.

Later as we retired, just before he closed his eyes to sleep, Elder Stevenson turned to me and said, "If I don't remember anything else, I want to remember how a man talks who really knows God."

"Me too, Elder."

We rose with the sun the following day, and long before noon we spotted their camp. As we approached them, we could see two men on either side of a fallen log and they looked like they were arm wrestling. They stopped when they saw us.

The younger of the two came straight up to me and gestured back at the other one.

"Does pretty good for a dead man, wouldn't you say? And an old one at that."

I grinned, "Yeah, he sure does."

"My name is Jonas," he offered. "And you must be Elders Jamison and Stevenson." He continued without missing a breath. "Samuel told me about you two. I guess he told you that I am to be assisting in your training for a couple of days."

He took each of us by the hand, one at a time and gave us each an extra enthusiastic, two handed handshake.

He didn't look like he was more than ten years older than we were. He was clean shaven, with short black hair, a quick smile and intense brown eyes. He stood about six feet even and had an average build.

Timothy was probably ten to fifteen years older than Jonas and you could tell they were related, as they looked like two pictures of the same person, taken a decade or two apart. Nephi, on the other hand looked to be five or ten years older than either Samuel or Seth.

That afternoon and evening, we were blessed with hearing, from his own lips, Nephi's account of all that had gone on from the prophecies of Samuel the Lamanite to the present. Incidentally, when he spoke of Samuel the Lamanite, he looked over and winked at Samuel, an act that was not lost on me, Elder Stevenson, or Seth. He spoke of the day and the night and the day that testified of the birth of Christ, and bore an overwhelming testimony of his confidence in Christ's coming.

He said quietly, "Most people have no idea how close to that day we really are."

Elder Stevenson and I knew, or at least by our accounts we did, and we fell asleep that night marveling to each other about our circumstances.

We were left alone for much of the next day as the four leaders met among themselves. We spent the time doing the best we could to recount to each other what we knew of the last few days of the Savior's life.

It was a completely unique experience to be thinking of those events, in what was for us, the present, only on the other side of the world.

"What a great story if they had CNN," I thought.

I remembered back to a book that my Seminary teacher had introduced me to. The name of the book was The Christ Commission, by Og Mandino. In it, he goes to great lengths to provide an educated guess and paint personality portraits of all the main people involved. With that memory, I had a vivid picture in my mind of all that might be happening about that time in Jerusalem.

I wanted desperately to tell Elder Stevenson about that book, but I was sure by then that he was from a time at least twenty years before Og Mandino wrote it.

After supper, we both took out our 'pocket formula' medallions and reviewed with each other all that we had been taught. We both agreed that where we came from, having something like that to carry with us would be a terrific reminder of where our thoughts should be.

"You know, Elder Jamison," he said thinking, "Seth mentioned that there had been quite a few from our dispensation that had been taught by him or Samuel or Jonas, didn't he?"

"Yes, I remember him saying that."

"Well, don't you wonder who they might have been?"

That question took us down a road of conversation that kept us speculating long after we should have gone to sleep and I thoroughly enjoyed every minute of it. History of any kind was exciting, but church history was a passion for both of us.

I don't think it necessarily was planned this way, but for an hour or so, earlier that evening, I was left to speak with Nephi and Seth by myself while Elder Stevenson spent the time with Samuel and Jonas. There were a million things that I wish, in hindsight, I would have asked them, but the experience was terrific still the same. I have no illusions that Nephi really looked like I remember him, but that beautiful, friendly, soft spoken face that I saw then, comes back to me every time I read Third Nephi.

I also wondered if he had been like Jonas when he

was younger. I like to think the enthusiasm and energy that Jonas had was a little like what I imagined Joseph Smith's personality to be like.

Samuel left us to go back to his own village the next morning. He took Elder Stevenson aside for a moment before he departed and had a few words with him. Even though my personal time the day before had been with Nephi and Seth, and I cherished it, I found myself a little jealous of my companion. There was something in Samuel that was very special and different and I really wish I'd have had the chance to get to know him better.

Jonas made arrangements for us to meet up with Seth and Nephi in two days or so, and then we left with him.

CHAPTER 9

The next couple of days with Jonas went very quickly. Each day he began by having an hour long discussion about that particular day's virtue. He started by having each of us give a thought, which we were supposed to have been thinking about in advance. He then went over the entire training agenda in detail. He started with the discussion on controlling our thoughts and ended by helping us understand more fully the goal-setting and follow-through process.

He asked questions constantly, and like Samuel, he was acutely interested in making sure that we knew how to teach each point. He was also an artist at framing his questions to stimulate careful thought.

He would listen to our answers patiently, replying with, "Uh huh," then a pause, or "OK, that might work." Then he would return with, "So if that's the case, how would it apply to this?"

He would continue that process on each issue until he was satisfied that we had covered all possible contingencies. It was truly exciting.

One thing about Jonas. He was much bolder and more blunt than either of the other two. It seemed to suit him, however, as neither of us ever felt the need to take offense. I remember one point that he made before he pronounced his part of the training finished.

"Young brothers," he said sternly as he looked us in the eyes, "in your discussions it is important to find common ground from which to begin teaching. But don't let the need for a common ground ever cloud your message. Never let the Lord hear you apologize for his gospel." I can still see his face in my mind as he said that and I have replayed it to myself many times.

We met up with Seth and Nephi again just before noon on Thursday in a little village about the size of Samuel's. The route we had taken must have been quite a bit longer than theirs, as they informed us that they had arrived the evening before.

As soon as we had finished a short lunch, Nephi asked Jonas to ready his animals. He said they were in quite a hurry, and asked Seth to meet up with them in Zarahemla when he had finished with us.

Just before they departed, Nephi walked to where Elder Stevenson and I were standing. He firmly put one hand on my shoulder and the other on my companion's, as he looked through our eyes, deep into our hearts.

"You are fine young men," he said softly. "And there are millions of people in your time that don't know that our world exists. They don't know that we believe in Christ, and it's likely that some of them don't want to know.

"You'll do all you can to change that, won't you?"

Speechless, we both just nodded.

Nephi then joined the others and they all smiled as they turned back and waved.

"Goodbye, Brother Seth, we'll see you soon. Goodbye, Elders."

That night as we knelt together, after Seth had offered the prayer, I surprised myself by asking the Lord if there was any way that I could stay there. It was such a time of anticipation. I was well aware of the events that were to shortly shake this world, but I also knew that the period of suffering was limited, and then they would see the Savior.

And I was also conscious of the beautiful harmony that would exist there in the very near future. If only I could.

I felt Seth's hand on my shoulder as I finished. He was standing between us and his other hand was on the shoulder of Elder Stevenson.

"You are both praying for the same thing, I think, and that makes me feel good," he sighed.

"But your work is back in your time, and it won't be long now. You heard Nephi tell me that I was to return to Zarahemla as soon as you both were finished. He also said earlier that you will be our last students for a while. It seems that other things will demand our attention soon."

As a summary he instructed: "Elders, I would ask you to remember all of the events of these past eleven days. Remember the formula for righteous development that is represented on your medallions, which is:

Step 1...Begin by keeping an eye single to the glory of God at all times.

Step 2...Prove and develop all virtues by the process known as Faith, Hope and Charity.

Step 3...Concentrate on increasing a particular virtue each day.

Step 4...Make your growth systematic by 'Growing by the season.'

Step 5...Take advantage of the Lord's promise by focusing your thoughts on virtue."

We sat there by the fire until long into the night. Both of us bore our testimonies to Seth and told him of our love for him. We were careful not to mention anything about our time, but we both bore witness that the promises made by way of prophesy that were to be fulfilled between his time and ours had all been fulfilled.

Elder Stevenson even joked a little and asked with a sly grin, "Are you sure you don't want to know something about our time and how the church is doing?"

"It would be nice," Seth replied, "but it's not permitted. And I know more about your time than you might think, just by watching you elders."

He then bore his testimony of the truthfulness of the Plan of Salvation and of his confidence in the resurrection of the Savior. He recounted again how he had been there as a young man with Nephi when the night never darkened and they were shown the sign of Christ's birth. He testified with simple dignity of the confidence he had in the teachings of his fathers. He spoke of Father Lehi and Nephi and added a little perspective that I had not thought of before.

He indicated that though the land of Jerusalem may have had the Savior for the past thirty three years, he was confident that his land would see him and hear him soon. And the one thing his land had that they did not, was the knowledge that the other land existed. He seemed to take a particular pride in that knowledge.

That observation made me smile.

I've thought many times since then how wonderful it would have been if we could have shared that experience with some of our investigators.

He then turned and walked over to get his bedroll. He paused, turned, and came back to us.

He took me by the hand, put his other hand on my shoulder, as he had done many times and said, looking me in the eye, "I love you, Elder Jamison." He did the same for Elder Stevenson and then looked directly at both of us and whispered, "And that love I feel for you two is not a dream."

After he went to sleep, Elder Stevenson and I sat

under that clear spring sky and talked about dozens of different topics. We spoke of how we both knew it would be ending soon and how we would miss each other.

I couldn't remember ever having a friend in my life that I had shared so much with, and with whom I had so much in common. We knew nothing about each other, yet we knew everything.

"Maybe," I thought hopefully, "he is real and we were friends in the pre-earth life." If that was the case, then I would indeed see him again. I just wished that I knew better about when and where he was from.

I had been quite positive for some time that he was from at least a generation before my time, but then a small slip confirmed it.

During that conversation, I put it to him, "Elder Stevenson, I was wondering just how old you are. You don't look much older than me, but you seem to be much more experienced than I am."

He smiled, "I'll be twenty four in six weeks. I got drafted and joined the Navy just before I turned nineteen, and if the Japanese hadn't of surrendered when they did, I'd probably still be there." He realized immediately what he had said and changed the subject, but I had the picture in my mind, and it was about what I had thought.

"Elder, do you think they would mind if I asked you if you had a girl waiting at home?" he asked.

"I don't see how it could do any harm," I smiled. "Girls are not unique to any generation, I don't think. But yes, I do. I wish I could show you a picture of her. How about you?"

"No, I did, but she's engaged to a friend now."

We continued talking like that for a few more minutes and then he got very emotional. He looked at me as if he'd known me forever and suggested, "No matter where you go back to or where I do, let's make a promise between us right now."

"What kind of a promise?" I asked.

"Let's promise to always remember each other. Whether you actually exist or will exist in my world or I in yours, let's never forget our friendship."

We took each other by the right hands, just as Seth had done, and put our left hands on each others shoulder, then he said clearly; "Wherever we go, whatever we do, Brothers Forever!"

"Brothers forever," I returned enthusiastically.

He put his arms around me and I put mine around him.

I tossed and turned constantly that night as I struggled to sleep. It seemed like a dream within a dream, but I remember tremendous thunder and lightning coming up all of a sudden. I heard a huge crack and saw the lightning at the same instant and then heard the explosion as a huge cottonwood tree was struck down the middle. The noise was deafening. And the wind. It seemed to come out of nowhere.

Everything was shaking violently and I felt like the earth was being torn apart beneath me. All at once the ground split and a huge crevice appeared, separating Elder Stevenson and me from where Seth was sleeping.

But he was gone. I looked through the darkness across the widening canyon. As the lightning filled the sky I could see that where he had been lying, there was nothing. No donkeys, no supplies, nothing.

The earth kept falling away in huge pieces into the crack. As I reached to wake Elder Stevenson, the ground beneath me gave way and I grasped in vain to catch hold of something.

"Elder Stevenson!" I cried. "Elder Stevenson!" I remember falling.

CHAPTER 10

I was awakened by Elder Mitchell shaking me.

"Boy, I didn't think I would ever get you up," he said as I opened my eyes. "You were totally out of it, and you better hurry; it's already after nine and we need to leave by nine thirty to make it to church in time."

I was still out of breath. I'd had dreams that seemed real before, but this time the return to reality didn't seem as real as the dream. I laid there on my bed collecting my thoughts for the next few minutes.

It was a real let down. Even as I was scrambling in my dream to keep from falling, I knew that what had happened meant that the Savior had died. It all made sense. And I was sure that Seth knew and had left us for the purpose of being where he should be at the proper time. I just hoped that both he and Elder Stevenson were all right.

"What was I thinking about?" I thought. Those events were only a dream and I had to snap out of it. I looked at the clock next to my bed, which now said 9:10 and, seeing that, I jumped out quickly and got into the shower.

I was still shaking inside with the memory as we turned the car onto the highway and headed south to Pontiac.

"Elder, who's Elder Stevenson?" my companion asked.

"What? Oh." I caught myself and replied, "He's the new elder coming in on Friday; I thought you knew."

"No, I didn't know that. I didn't think they told you which one you were getting. The reason I asked is that you were calling to an Elder Stevenson in your sleep, just before you woke up."

I really didn't want to get into my dream right then, so I simply said, "He was probably on my mind because President Patterson said that was the name of my new companion, that's all."

"By the way," he said to change the subject, "The assistants called while you were in the shower. They said they wanted to talk to you about your new elder. They said they'd call back tonight, though."

All through Sacrament meeting and Brother Hardy's Sunday School class I kept thinking about my dream. I went over in my mind the entire sequence of events and the points that Seth had taught us. I was certain that it hadn't happened by chance and I wished that there was a way of knowing if Seth had ever existed. Knowing I wasn't going to find anything, I still turned to Third Nephi and scanned through the pages looking for the mention of his name.

One thing I did find that was exciting, however, was that Jonas was also called as a disciple, along with Nephi and Timothy.

And then there was Elder Stevenson, and as much as I had grown to love him, that had to have been just a name I put into my dream because of my new assignment. "Still the same," I thought, "someday at the genealogical library, I'm going to dig deep into the Stevenson name." I knew that as I had promised, I would never forget him.

Thinking to myself, I remembered the points I had been taught in detail. "Control my thoughts. Keep an eye single to the glory of God. 'The three degrees of devotion,' faith, hope and charity. 'The six essential missionary virtues;' Knowledge, Patience, Diligence, Humility, Brotherhood and Godliness, along with their supporting virtues. 'Living by the Season,' and that wonderful promise."

I found myself opening my scriptures to the note pages and tracing a circle on the page. I put a hexagon within the circle and a triangle within the hexagon. I then drew a small sun in the middle. So simple, I thought.

I resolved to write down everything that I had been taught. If I was going to have a dream about people that may or may not have been real, at least the change in my life would be real.

I felt guilty, though, as I found myself wishing that Elder Stevenson was sitting there in Priesthood Meeting with me instead of Elder Mitchell.

"What a wonderful guy," I thought, regardless of whether he was real or not.

I did write it all down that evening. I stayed up much longer than I should have, but I didn't want to forget a single detail. I began to formulate a plan then, one that I could use to get myself on track.

I even cut a piece of cardboard into a circle about the size of a silver dollar and drew the 'Pocket Formula' that I had seen in my dream. I remembered everything word for word that was represented except the promise on the back. I knew the essence of it but I could not get the words the way Seth had said them.

After I had written down all that I could remember, I put my papers away, knelt down and prayed.

I explained to the Lord all that had happened, as if

he didn't know. I thanked him for caring enough about me to let me learn in this way. I then asked him for all of the strength he could give me. I wanted more than anything to make myself worthy of what I now felt my mission was.

When I was through, I crawled into bed and opened my scriptures. The chapter I turned to was the one hundred and twenty-first section of the D&C and I began to read. When I got to the part where it said, Many are called but few are chosen, I knew I had my theme for that season. I got out of bed and wrote down, Season #1: The season I choose to become chosen.

Then another thought hit me as I read the forty-fifth verse.

...And let virtue garnish thy thoughts unceasingly, then shall thy confidence wax strong in the presence of God, and the Doctrine of the Priesthood shall distil upon thy soul as the dews from heaven.

And I knew what to write on the back of my cardboard 'Pocket Formula.'

From that day on, following the rules and learning the gospel was a joy. There was nothing else in the world as far as I was concerned. I began to formulate a theme for the following season, as the one I began was a shortened one.

I used the theme, A Season for Sharing, as my focus for the following season. I made a commitment to share the principles on the medallion and the 'Growing by the Season,' technique with one new elder each week. I had to get creative at first, because I was not always in close enough contact with other elders.

Elder Taylor, my Zone leader, was one of the first that I shared it with. He was wonderful and loved the idea of the 'Pocket Formula.' He and his companion made their own and then he enlisted my help in teaching it to the rest of the zone.

The one thing that Elder Taylor told me was that as he tracked the follow-through, the elders that were setting their goals quarterly had nearly twice the rate of completing their scripture reading.

Incidentally, during those last thirteen months, I finished the Book of Mormon twice, the New Testament once and the Doctrine and Covenants and the Pearl of Great Price once each. I had not completed even one up until that time.

CHAPTER 11

As for my new companion, one of the Assistants did call that Sunday evening.

"Elder Jamison, this is Elder Jensen. I'm calling to tell you the name of your new companion."

I answered quickly, "President Patterson already told me last Thursday who it would be. He said it would be Elder Stevenson."

He must have thought I was joking with him because he laughed, and then he replied, "Well, I don't know where you got that from, but it wasn't from the President. He said he mentioned that he didn't know yet who it would be. By the way, your new companion's name is Elder Lance Call, and I'm sorry, Elder, but there isn't even an Elder Stevenson in the group."

I had been so certain of his name. Of course that had been a lifetime ago, in my dream. I guess that through self-suggestion I could have inserted the name of the elder in my dream and applied it to him.

"OK," I said, still confused. "By the way, I won't let you or the President down, you'll see. I have been studying hard and I'm going to do things right."

I guess he could sense a new conviction in my voice, because he said, "That's great, Elder; that's exactly what we wanted to hear."

Anyway, Elder Call arrived by bus late in the afternoon on Friday. When I saw him, for whatever reason, I knew I was going to like him. One problem, though, was that he was deathly homesick. His family had not been able to see him off at the airport. A huge snowstorm had closed both roads out of his hometown so they hadn't been able to come and say goodbye. This was his first time away from home, and now three weeks after leaving for the MTC, he was sure that he had made a big mistake. After we got his bags in he just sat there on the bed and cried.

"Elder Jamison," he sobbed, "I really don't know why I'm here. My mother and Grandmother need me, and if I was home I could be enrolled in school now, as well."

It was sad to watch how he was hurting as he continued. "Up until my grandfather died, all he ever talked about was me going on a mission and I made the mistake of promising him that I would. My mother and Grandmother convinced me that it would be OK, but I know now that I only came because I felt compelled to come. I want to go home, Elder."

He was in real tough shape, and my heart just ached for what he was feeling. Two weeks earlier I would have been tempted to just let him alone to sort it all out, but with the renewed life I felt, I just hit him with both barrels.

"Elder Call," I said enthusiastically, "cheer up guy, and come over here." I then had him stand there facing me, belly to belly, looking me in the eye, and I said, "it's face-off time."

I first had him clench his fists and put them up in front of him like Elder Stevenson had done in my dream. Then I had him rest the back of his fists on my chest, so that no knuckles would make contact. Then I did the same.

I showed him gently how it was done and then told him, "Every time you get gloomy, I'm going to have you face-off with me like this. We will start beating each other's chest till one of us laughs. The one who laughs first is the loser."

I know it sounds really childish, but it had worked for Elder Stevenson and me.

What I found out the hard way, was that he had done that before. We stood there for nearly a minute, hammering on each other and biting our tongues until he had just about pounded a hole in me.

I began to laugh out loud and stammered, "You win, you win."

He began to laugh with me, and for the next couple of hours we got to know each other. I found out that he had been raised in Randolph, Utah, until his father had died. His mother then took him with her to live with his grandparents in Wyoming. And then just last year, shortly after his eighteenth birthday, his grandfather had passed away.

He was a dyed in the wool Aggie fan. His father had gone to Utah State and he was planning on attending there when he got home. He also said he wanted to study history, which put us both on the same wave length instantly, Aggie or no Aggie.

He claimed that he was an excellent cook. That particular statement I came to find out was not just an idle boast. I ended up doing dishes for nearly every meal as my part of the deal, but it was worth it to eat his cooking.

At ten o'clock, I asked him to sit down with me so we could plan our next day.

"Here's how we'll start, Elder," I said. "First thing you need to be thinking about is your goals for the next three months. By Sunday, you need to decide on a 'Theme' and your primary scripture reading.

"The reading is pretty much spelled out in your missionary training manual and I'll try to help you with the theme this time.

"Now because tomorrow is Saturday, our virtue for the day is Godliness. In our reading tonight and in our personal study in the morning, let's each find one thought that pertains to Godliness that we can share with each other; fair enough?"

His lip quivered a little and then he asked, "Elder Jamison, can I tell you something?"

"Sure, Elder, go ahead."

"Elder, I have been so depressed since I left the MTC on Wednesday. I studied hard for that three weeks, I really did. I learned each principle they taught. I know most of my discussions as well, but I was scared. It didn't hit me until I got to the airport. As I started thinking of leaving my mother and grandmother for two years, I just couldn't take it. I really began to believe that I was only here out of obligation to my grandfather. I even asked President Patterson to send me home last night. I don't really know how he talked me into taking the bus up here to meet you.

"And I know this sounds crazy, but when you told me to face-off with you, I knew everything would be all right. That's the thing my grandfather used to do with me to cheer me up. Of course, he stopped as I grew older and bigger and he grew older and weaker."

"I figured you had done that before," I said, as I gingerly rubbed my bruised chest.

He went on. "And your description of how you set goals, and your identifying a certain virtue each day, he used to do that, too. He would turn to the fourth section of the D&C and tell me, work on one of these each day and you'll never be led astray. He even had little wooden medallions made up for the Priests in our stake to help them remember."

I started to get goosebumps about then.

"In fact," he said as he went over to his suitcase, "I've still got one of them."

Then I about lost it.

As he pulled out a round wooden coin, about the size of the wooden nickels they used to throw out at the parades, I started to quiver.

"This can't be," I thought.

On the front was the same design. A sun inside of a triangle, inside of a hexagon. The same words were there, too. On the back he had printed the last part of the thirteenth article of faith.

If there is anything virtuous, lovely, or of good report, or praiseworthy, we seek after these things.

Feeling a little shaken, I pulled the cardboard disc out of my jacket pocket and showed it to him. He never finished what he was saying; he just threw his arms around me and said, "Thanks, Elder."

We were together for two months, and they were the most exciting two months of my life. As we both struggled to learn together, I found that each night when I went to bed, the most exciting thing on my mind was tomorrow.

Being with him also helped me to live in the present and quit daydreaming about my time with Elder Stevenson, as I had done constantly for the first few days after my dream. Only when I pulled out my pocket formula, or gave in to Elder Call's challenge to 'face-off,' did I find myself missing him.

You know, I never did win one with Elder Call. For a kid that had started in such an emotional way, he was tough as nails.

I did ask him once if he knew where his grandfather came up with the idea for his coin, but he couldn't remember if he had ever been told.

It just seemed like too big of a coincidence.

And I never did tell anyone about my dream. That was between me and the Lord. That is, until I told President Patterson one night after a fireside.

I really didn't know how he would take it, but he took it very well, and even encouraged me to document it in detail, which I had already done.

One other thing. I know this might sound a little odd, but here's the other motivator that I carried with me from then on.

Elder Jamison kept on talking as he dug into his planner.

"Mom, do you remember asking me to take a picture of myself with each of my companions? Well, first off, I'm glad that you did.

"But take a look at this picture."

Rick handed them a picture of himself. It was just one half of a snap-shot, but that half was glued to a 3X5 card, leaving the right side blank. In the blank area, he had written the words,

Elder Jamison and Elder Stevenson
"Brothers Forever"
November, 1997

"I had Elder Call take this picture of me while I was standing next to a tree. I cut it in half and, well, you see. I know it sounds strange, but it saved me many times. Each time I felt discouraged with a companion or with myself, I just took out that picture and immediately had to smile.

"It had never occurred to me to ask Elder Call the name of his grandfather until I was on the plane coming home. I know it's highly unlikely, but I am going to write and ask him just the same.

"Well, that's my story. I'd like to think that the things in my dream really existed somewhere, but it doesn't matter. What does matter is that I found out that the principles and techniques work."

Elder Jamison's mother was crying and his father was just nodding his head and beaming. Sister Jensen looked over at her cousin, who was searching for a handkerchief in her purse.

President Jensen smiled big and said, "Son, you are truly a choice young man. Never, ever, let that memory die."

He then got up and walked over to Rick's chair.

"Would you mind if we release you now?"

"That would be fine, President."

He then laid his hands on Rick's head and released him. He also gave him a blessing and a bit of counsel.

One statement that Rick remembered was,

"Rick, you have been given a special gift, and a special manifestation of how that gift should be used. In due time, all the pieces to the puzzle now in your mind will be put in their proper place."

After he was done, President Jensen motioned behind his back for Sister Jensen's cousin to come over.

She walked slowly over to Rick and looked into his eyes. Tears began to flow as she nodded.

"Yes, I am sure of it," she sobbed.

"Elder Jamison, I am honored to finally meet you," and she gently squeezed his hand.

"And yes, I am Sister Jensen's cousin. I wrote to her

a few months back to inquire about you and when I found out when you would be returning, I asked them if I could come and meet you."

"For you see, I am your Elder Call's grandmother.

"And. . .

"I am also Elder Stevenson's wife."

Rick's heart stopped cold.

"I thought you might like this."

Then she handed him a picture. It was an old black and white snapshot, pasted on a mat, cut in half, with the left half removed, and an outline around the missing half.

It was a picture of Elder Stevenson!

Within the outline were written the words,

Elder Stevenson and Elder Jamison
"Brothers Forever"
April, 1946
